MW01247095

Long Journey Home

Nancy Silvers

Script A Life Books

Waterville, Ohio

Journey Home Series

Long Journey Home

A Second Chance

One More Mile

No More Strings

Kingdom Come

Walking Through the Valley

Green Pastures

The Winds of Change

Valley of Decision

One Final Glimpse Backward

Script A Life Books
Waterville, Ohio 43566
Scriptalife.com

The only journey

is

the journey

within.

Rainer Maria Rilke

Chapter One

The afternoon sun streamed through the trees, haloing soldier and horse below as they traveled beneath the trees' thick canopy. Light and shadow played awhile on the soldier's shoulders as he regarded the woods around him, noting spring had come to the South. The forest wore rich greens and browns, a vibrant backdrop to the pastel dogwoods and pale wildflowers lining the road. Acknowledging the color and fragrant air approvingly, the soldier found both invigorating after the bleak war years.

Leaving the woods, he and his mare entered a plain of verdant meadows where sunshine quickly enveloped them, its warmth relaxing the soldier's shoulders as it penetrated his wool coat. While his mare sauntered beneath him, he reached inside his coat pocket and pulled out a letter from his brother written at the end of the war.

September 1, 1865

Dear Gideon,

I hope this letter reaches you soon. When I was mustered out of the infantry last week, I made haste for home, arriving just two days ago. It is a peculiarity to reach home at last only to find Mother and Father in the burial mounds on the hill. Never drew breath any finer parents than we had, Gideon. With the terrible conflict over, it is indeed grievous to come home to more sadness.

Leaning forward, Gideon patted his mare as he pictured his brother on their Ohio farm standing at their parents' graves. At least Tom was there, back on the land they loved. Unfortunately the Federal hospitals had not vacated as fast as the Federal ranks. Wistful all of a sudden, Gideon soberly returned his attention to the letter.

I am keeping right busy, and you will be most heartened to know the farm is in good hands now that I am home. The air breathes more freely here. Yet with our President gone, there lingers a sadness that makes difficult any real thoughts of optimism. Mr. Lincoln was unpopular with many, but I believed him to be a good man who inspired us through the darkest hours of the war. I know you feel the same.

Biting his lip, Gideon glanced up from the letter as he recalled Mr. Lincoln's speech in Cincinnati in '59 that had first inspired him and Tom before the 1860 election. In answer to President Lincoln's call for volunteers in '61 to end the rebellion, he and his best friend Penn along with Tom had eagerly enlisted. Never did they imagine the conflict would take so long, however, and end with a Northern victory so hollow after President Lincoln's assassination. But the rebellion *was* over, Gideon gratefully acknowledged. Lifting a hand to shield his eyes from the sun, he focused again on the letter.

I know they will not let you go quickly since the pressing need of the wounded lingers long past the rebels' surrender, and I know there are no limits to your wanting to help in any capacity you are able. Still, when you are mustered out, hasten home. There is a place waiting for you here. Proceed with caution, however. The terrible conflict may have ended, but broken lives do not heal quickly. God speed your journey home.

Tom

Returning the letter to his pocket, Gideon regarded the emerging spring around him.

"Won't be too long now, Red, till we are back in Cincinnati. Then we can put the hospitals and rebels behind us," Gideon encouraged as his spirits lifted with hope.

Hope. It seemed a foreign emotion after long years of war.

Brushing back a shock of hair, he pictured again the family farm. His entire constitution had been neglected serving on battlefields and in Federal hospitals since '61, so he vowed quietly to take better care of himself when he got home, feeling sure the hours behind a plow would put things right again. Turning his attention to the resurgence of life around him, he suddenly got the urge for a gallop.

"Come on, Red. Let's cut those miles to

home."

Picking up her gait responsively, the mare accelerated into a sprint across the greening land, causing her rider's blue eyes to soften and his lips to pull back into a smile. With mane and coattails whipped back, they made a graceful pair as they sped past flowering meadows in rhythmic union. When they entered another dense woods, however, the mare dramatically slowed her gait, tripping in the process and catapulting her rider into the air. Responding with a life-saving tuck, Gideon landed hard.

With injured foreleg Red regarded her fallen rider from the road and watched for movement while quiet settled in the woods around them. Nuzzling against Gideon's neck, she got no response so she raised her head and whinnied before nuzzling him again. This time she was rewarded when he stirred and slowly turned over onto his back.

Opening his eyes, Gideon took a moment to focus. Able to gain a sitting position after a few minutes, he brushed back his disheveled hair and quickly pulled his hand away with a grimace, noting blood on his palm. With a frown he retrieved his kerchief and pressed it against a cut above his eye while he gingerly checked his body for more injuries. Finding all apparently intact, he tried to stand until his right knee buckled. Feeling faint, he eased himself back down onto the ground and pressed the kerchief again to his head.

"We sure did it up right this time, Red," he declared, glancing up to the mare.

Raising her head, Red whinnied as Gideon planted his hands behind him on the grass and tried to focus.

"My sentiments exactly, girl," he muttered, blinking again to clear his vision as he leaned forward to check his injured knee.

Relieved to find it not broken, he quietly diagnosed the injury a bad sprain. Noticing a large branch on the ground near him, he used the branch to gain his feet again, ignoring his knee's painful protest and the returning dizziness. When his vision cleared, he glanced around him to get his bearings.

The mountains lay behind him. He knew he did not want to go there. Not sure where he was exactly, he felt certain that for a Northerner, it was nowhere safe. Wishing now he had left for home when the rest of the Federal troops had departed, he glanced down at his clothes. Although dressed as a civilian, he knew enough Union ties still remained about him and his horse that any observant Southerner could detect. Using the branch now as a crutch, he took a step toward Red and noticed her favoring her foreleg. With a sigh he stroked her nose and glanced around them warily.

"This isn't good, Red. It is not good at all."

Using the branch, he tried taking a few steps but had to stop.

"Gideon Taylor, you have really gotten yourself into a fix this time," he admonished as he squinted up against the indifferent sun.

When he dropped his gaze to the road ahead, he thought he saw a signpost in a moment of clearing vision.

"Come on, girl. Maybe help isn't that far away."

* * *

Braxton Springs - 2 miles, Gideon read before his vision blurred again. A faded arrow on the sign pointed west so he directed his gaze accordingly and stared down the western road to his left. With a sigh he regarded the sign again, focusing on the faded print. It had been an ordeal making it to the signpost so he doubted he could go another two miles. What Southern town would help a Federal soldier anyway? He patted his mare next to him and glanced again to her foreleg. What he desired most for them both was rest, a dangerous option.

Suddenly Red whinnied.

"What is it, girl?" Gideon asked, stroking her nose as he listened quietly a moment. "I hear it, Red," he responded with a smile. "Come on."

Hobbling awkwardly through flowering dogwoods and tangling underbrush, the pair made their way to the most welcoming stream, its flowing water drawing them to its edge. Gratefully easing down onto the bank, Gideon drank with cupped hands, relishing the spring water.

"Maybe this day won't turn out so bad after

all, Red," Gideon observed, soaking his kerchief in the stream while Red drank next to him.

Applying the wet cloth to the wound above his eye, Gideon grimaced. When he submerged the kerchief into the water to rinse, his eyes fixed themselves on the crimson cloth as his surroundings faded. Hearing a familiar voice imploring him to save a leg, Gideon frowned as a cacophony of other soldiers' cries drowned out the first one. Distraught, he placed a hand to his head, hopelessly lost as his mind pulled him back to the Federal field hospitals, entrapping him there.

Nuzzling against him, Red waited until Gideon finally returned to the present. When he noticed the mare at last, he stroked her nose and finished rinsing before easing himself back against a tree. Holding the wet kerchief to his injured knee, he considered constructing makeshift splints to give it support. Too weary to think very long about it, he turned his attention to Red's injured foreleg, leaning forward to check it more closely. Red protested with a snort, stepping away from him. Giving up on the examination, he leaned back against the tree.

"I know. We are both in a mess here. I just have to figure out what to do."

Closing his eyes, Gideon listened awhile to the soothing sound and cadence of the lively stream. Dozing off, he awoke with a start awhile later and noticed with concern that the sun had dipped considerably, its position almost level now with the trees. With consternation he also sensed he was not alone. Glancing to his left, he stared into a rifle barrel while another cocked to his right.

Chapter Two

"Don't move, or you're a dead man," warned the man on his left.

Glancing to the man, Gideon noted the dirt-covered pants and tattered flannel shirt before focusing on the man's hair and face. Almost comical in appearance, the lank man's hair spread out from his head in snakelike clusters like Medusa.

"Look, here, Matthew. We come into the woods fer game and trapped us a real prize," the man on Gideon's right giddily announced, issuing forth the most idiotic laugh Gideon had ever heard.

Moving his gaze to the idiotic laugher, Gideon noticed the man's dress seemed very similar to Medusa's.

"Yeah, Matthew. Ma will be real pleased,"

Medusa added as Gideon turned his attention to the third stranger, the one the other two had addressed as Matthew.

Attired like his brothers, Matthew's face reflected an intelligence seemingly absent in the other two and a demeanor much more sullen as he crouched down in front of Gideon.

"What ya doin' here?" Matthew bellowed, eyeing Gideon intently.

Gideon gave no reply.

"Ya best be givin' us a good answer," Matthew demanded, rising to his feet.

"Going home," Gideon answered quietly, concealing his Northern accent.

"Mighty nice horse ya got there," Medusa taunted.

"Yeah, much too good for the likes of this stranger, wouldn't ya say, Chauncey?" the idiotic laugher chimed in, his spit showering Gideon's coat as he talked.

Gideon frowned. The crude brothers smelled of liquor and outnumbered him three to one.

Unfortunately his one did not count for much at that point. Stifling panic, Gideon struggled to think as he watched Medusa advance to Red. More than a horse to him, Red was not going to be taken by these men if he could help it. When Medusa grabbed Red's reins, Gideon's jaw tightened. He started to rise until the idiotic laugher's rifle poked into his ribs, pinning him to the tree.

"Matthew, ain't these Yankee saddlebags?" Medusa observed, removing the bags from the mare.

Joining his brother, Matthew ran his finger over the imprinted "U.S." on the leather bags before inspecting their contents. Although unable to read the Federal papers he found, he recognized the same "U.S." written repeatedly on them. When he spied a handful of medals as well, his eyes narrowed.

"Who are ya, Mister?" Matthew demanded, glancing angrily back to Gideon.

"I'd say he's a Yankee, Matthew," Medusa observed, spitting with contempt.

Unsure how to respond, Gideon remained quiet as the men approached. Acutely aware of the hopelessness of his situation, Gideon knew there was nothing he could do but brace for the inevitable. Fleetingly he thought of Tom and their Ohio farm he would probably never see again as Matthew jerked him up onto his feet and forcefully drove his fist into his abdomen. Before Gideon could recover, Medusa's fist met his face, sending him back against the tree. Then the idiotic laugher began pummeling his fists into Gideon as well. In the midst of it all, Gideon's knee pulsed pain as he felt himself sinking slowly into a welcome oblivion.

Suddenly all became quiet. The beating had stopped. Lying in a heap on the ground, Gideon took in short, painful breaths as he struggled to see. Wiping the blood from his eye, he noticed a fourth man had joined the brothers. Clad in buckskin, the stranger towered above the others and seemed to be sizing up the situation as his grizzled, bearded face clouded with anger.

"Ya varmits. Ya've been messin' with ma traps agin," the man hollered, eyeing the brothers' animal-laden horses. "Don't try lyin' neither. I tracked ya here."

"Now, Caleb, it ain't the way it appears here," Matthew lied, clearly intimidated by the man. "We come across this Yankee here, and he was the one who was messin' with yore traps. We caught 'im fer ya and was givin' 'im what he deserves. The animals there was on his horse when we come upon 'im."

Impressed with their brother's lie, Medusa and the idiotic laugher issued eager nods and motioned toward Gideon's horse. Glancing responsively to the mare, Caleb also eyed Gideon a moment before leveling his rifle again at the brothers.

"Ya Bunch brothers never could do nothin' right, especially lyin'. Now git outta here before I fill yer hides with lead," Caleb ordered.

"But the Yankee?" Matthew protested.

"Leave 'im. And leave ma animals."

Hurriedly the brothers obeyed, moving the stolen game onto Caleb's mule before mounting their horses and reluctantly riding away. After they left, Caleb turned back to Gideon.

"I didn't do what they said, Mister," Gideon

protested weakly as Caleb's powerful arms lifted him to his feet. Too weak to resist, Gideon collapsed against the man.

"Dab nabit. I don't need this," Caleb snarled, lowering Gideon to the ground.

* * *

The picture on the wall blurred and became clear again. Gideon's head was pounding, but he tried to focus on his surroundings. He was lying in a soft bed oddly enough with plump, comforting pillows and a patterned quilt. He was also wearing a nightshirt not his own, and when he placed his hand to his head, he could feel some neatly-done stitches above his eye. When he moved, every bone and muscle in his body seemed to ache. It even hurt to breathe. Closing his eyes, he grimaced.

Moments later he opened his eyes and looked around him again, noting the welcome breeze afforded him through an open window. When he caught a glimpse of a glass of water on a bedside table, he swallowed hard. Every move was taxing, but his mouth felt so dry. With great effort he clasped the glass, his hand shaking responsively. Surprised by his weakness, he watched helplessly as the glass slipped out of his hand, shattering into pieces on the floor. When the door to his room opened moments later, he attempted to sit up until dizziness drove him back onto the pillow. Putting a hand to his head, he closed his eyes.

"I'm sorry," he offered softly when he heard someone approaching the bed.

There was no response.

Then he heard glass.

"I am sorry," he repeated a little louder.

"Shh!" came a female response.

Opening his eyes, Gideon looked toward the window but saw nothing so he concluded he must be dreaming until a woman stood up next to the bed, holding the broken shards in her apron. Noting her form, he tried to focus.

"You must be quiet," she admonished in a soft Southern drawl.

"I really am sorry," he responded quietly, closing his eyes again.

Receiving his apology skeptically, she regarded him a moment.

When is the last time he gazed at his reflection in the looking glass? she wondered, noting the length of his disheveled blond hair.

Although apprehensive, she dared herself to linger a minute longer. When Caleb had brought the stranger to the back door after supper, her Uncle Nathan had not hesitated to give him shelter. Her uncle's habit of taking in the lost, however, seemed to have gone too far this time. He had even convinced Josiah to take the stranger's horse to his livery. Biting her lip pensively, she continued her observation until Gideon emitted a soft groan. Instinctively she took a step closer and felt his forehead, noting its warmth as his eyes opened in response to her cool hand. Promptly removing her hand, she noticed the vibrant blue of his eyes.

"Could I have a drink please?"

Yes, of course. I will go fetch a glass for you

now. You must not make another sound, however. No one must know you are here," she answered.

Hearing the bedroom door opening behind her, she drew in an anxious breath and clutched her apron more tightly as she turned toward the sound.

CHAPTER THREE

"Uncle Nathan, what are you doing up here? What about your patients downstairs?" the young woman admonished, spying him in the doorway.

The good-natured doctor held up his hand in response.

"Patients are gone so I figure we have ourselves a little breather. Would you mind bringing my supper up here, Abigail? That way I can check on our patient and eat at the same time."

With a nod Abigail moved toward the door. When she passed her uncle, he spied her glass-laden apron and placed a hand on her arm, causing her to stop.

"That what caused all the noise?"

"Yes. He knocked a glass off the table. His forehead feels warm. I was about to get him more water. I will bring your supper too," she reported before continuing to the door.

"Thought I saw an apple pie cooling on the windowsill this afternoon," Nathan remarked, trying to cajole her with his good humor. Seeing her pause in the doorway, he smiled when she turned back to him."You know it is my favorite, Abigail."

Abigail glanced to Gideon.

"Well, I am not certain if you deserve a piece or not, Uncle Nathan, allowing this trouble to come into our house."

"This isn't trouble, Abigail. It is just being a Good Samaritan. Isn't that what Reverend Johnson was preaching about last Sunday?"

"The Good Samaritan didn't have to cope with the trouble we will have if someone discovers we are harboring a Yankee in our house."

Nathan stifled a smile.

"Will you also bring some laudanum when you return?"

With an acknowledging nod she exited the room while Nathan approached the bed. Although tired, he immediately focused on his patient who seemed to be watching his every move. As he felt Gideon's forehead, he confirmed its warmth before examining Gideon's stitches over his eye.

"Are you a doctor?"

"Yes, son. I am Nathan Lawrence."

"Where am I?"

"In my home. I am the doctor here in Braxton Springs."

"Braxton Springs?"

"Yes, that is right. A very quiet little town filled with mighty good people."

Throwing back the quilt, Nathan took note of Gideon's grimaces with each examining touch.

"Caleb brought you here last night. Said he came upon you and the Bunch brothers about two miles up the road. He had tracked them there. They were messing with his traps. Not very smart to mess with ole Caleb."

Finished with the examination, Nathan threw the quilt back over Gideon and anchored down in the chair next to the bed.

"I would say you are a very lucky man. If Caleb hadn't come along when he did, God knows what the Bunch brothers would have done to you."

"Caleb?" Gideon repeated, trying to process the doctor's information.

"Local mountain man in these parts. Hardly ever comes to town. People are too noisy and nosey, he says. Keeps to himself most of the time. Yes, it is a work of Providence he came upon you when he did. Are you hungry?"

Gideon shook his head.

"Do you know what happened to my horse?"

"The local blacksmith has your mare down at the livery. He was visiting last night when Caleb brought you to the back door. Josiah will take good care of her for you."

As Gideon issued a relieved sigh, Nathan regarded him thoughtfully.

"I think you will be feeling fine, son, after a good dose of rest. Nothing appears to be broken."

"I am just grateful you took me in," Gideon answered, dropping his gaze to the quilt as he fingered it absently. "Don't know how I will repay you though."

Nathan smiled.

"No need. It is the least I could do for a fellow doctor."

Gideon's face registered surprise.

"I hope you don't mind. I went through your saddlebags," Nathan explained. "I don't normally meddle in a man's private affairs, mind you, but we had to know who you are."

Gideon's face clouded.

"You are Gideon Taylor, surgeon with the Federal army. Am I right?"

"I was. Not any more."

Puzzled by Gideon's response, Nathan pondered again what he had found in Gideon's saddlebags as Abigail returned.

Placing her uncle's food tray on his lap, Abigail removed Gideon's glass of water from the tray and turned to the bed while Gideon watched her, his vision clearing enough for him to see her more distinctly. When she helped him take a drink, he noted the refreshing scent of lavender.

These are good people, he acknowledged silently as he leaned back with a grimace onto the pillow.

Noting Gideon's discomfort, Nathan placed his supper tray on the bed.

"Give me the glass, Abigail," Nathan instructed, drawing up alongside her. "Did you bring the laudanum?"

"Yes," she answered, retrieving the bottle for him.

After preparing a medicinal dose, Nathan lifted Gideon's head as Abigail stepped aside and watched.

"Drink this, Gideon. It will help you rest," he urged.

With a nod Gideon complied.

Lingering by the bed, Nathan watched until Gideon began drifting off to sleep. With a motion to his niece, he retrieved his supper tray and quietly accompanied her to the door.

"And what about your supper?" she asked,

pausing in the doorway.

"I guess I will have to eat my supper with you," Nathan teased softly, relaxing into his casual manner.

"Not necessarily," she responded as they proceeded into the hallway.

Nathan turned to her, his eyebrow lifted.

"Josiah Peters is downstairs. I invited him again to supper," she explained.

"You did, did you?"

"Yes, I did. Now please don't go scaring him off this evening, Uncle Nathan."

"Scare him off? I will be on my best behavior," he promised, suppressing a smile.

* * *

The Bunch family cabin was located in a remote place far from town, and the family frequented Braxton Springs about as often as old Caleb, holding to much the same sentiments as his about civilization. Arriving home late after their assault on the Yankee, the Bunch brothers knew they could not arrive empty-handed so they had actually done some hunting. Successful in bringing home game for supper, they worked in the yard with their kill while their sister Martha watched from the porch. Staring through matted hair, the ten-year-old had spent most of her young life being an intent spectator in a world of illiterate men and a domineering mother.

Sarah Bunch, the family matriarch, rocked on the porch near Martha. Puffing her pipe, Sarah was as tough as any man and ruled her family with fear and intimidation. Even her grown sons cowered before her when she unleashed one of her verbal tirades. Coming home with game though had given the men confidence since Sarah was a hard taskmaster.

"Ma, we sure done good, didn' we?" Chauncey, the Medusa-haired brother, offered, his wide grin showing his confidence.

"Yeah, Ma, these here is the best we done brung ya yet," Seth added, letting out one of his idiotic laughs.

Matthew looked up from his work. Often a

burden to him, his brothers never seemed very bright. As a result his mother naturally always looked to him which meant a heavy load at times.

"We'd a had even more if we hadn't been sidetracked by that Yankee," Chauncey impulsively added.

Sarah stopped rocking mid-puff. Leaning forward, her face became severe.

"What did ya say?" she barked.

"We run into a Yankee. We'd a killed him too if old man Caleb hadn't a chased us off," Seth answered for Chauncey.

Sensing a storm coming, Matthew moved uncomfortably as Sarah, still spry for her sixty years, leaped to her feet and left the porch, striding toward her sons.

"What in tarnation are they a talkin' about, Matthew?" she demanded, her eyes boring into him.

"We met up with a Yankee along the road a piece. We beat him up real bad though, Ma. He must be dead by now," Matthew offered apologetically.

"He *must* be dead?" Sarah mocked as she

circled him. "He *must* be dead?"

Matthew involuntarily cringed. He knew he and his brothers were treading on dangerous ground. Their older brother Abel had died in the war, and while Abel's death had hit them all hard, his mother had never gotten over it.

"Where's the body then?" Sarah challenged. "Show it ta me."

"We ain't rightly got it, Ma," Chauncey answered timidly.

Sarah whacked him with her cane.

"Ow! Ma," Chauncey howled.

"Git. All of ya, git. And don't come back here without that Yankee. Do ya hear?"

Like obedient boys the men scattered to their horses and mounted quickly, giving one backward glance to their mother while Martha watched with mouth agape.

CHAPTER FOUR

"Abigail, may I help?" Josiah offered, rising from his chair in the kitchen after supper.

Nathan glanced up from his coffee.

"You can help me, Josiah, by sitting down there and helping us figure out what to do with that Yankee upstairs," Abigail replied from the dry sink.

"I don't know what to tell you," Josiah replied, compliantly taking his seat as Nathan stifled a smile. "I'm willing to keep his horse like I told you before, but I can't keep him at my place. When Caleb brought him to your porch last night, I just figured he'd be staying here with you."

"And you thought right, Josiah," Nathan interjected. "He is much too weak to be talking about moving him."

With a scowl Abigail glanced back to her uncle.

"You are impossible sometimes, Uncle Nathan. We can't keep him upstairs much longer."

Unmoved, Nathan sipped his coffee as his niece turned back to the dishes. After another sip he focused again on Josiah. An expert smithy and Braxton Springs' most eligible bachelor, Josiah with his affable ways and good looks proved a desirable prospect for the single women in town who repeatedly vied for his attention at every town social. Although Abigail had obviously stolen his heart, his admirers noticed her seeming indifference to his attentions, keeping their hopes alive even though he seemed unmoved by her aloofness.

"How is the soldier's horse faring, Josiah?" Nathan asked.

"It will take awhile, but the mare should be all right. I'm keepin' her still in a stall to help her heal."

"Just like we are doing for her rider," Nathan observed with a smile.

Wiping her hands on her apron, Abigail turned to her uncle with a frown as Josiah rose to pull out a chair for her at the table. When she moved to be seated, a shout sounded from upstairs - the Yankee's.

* * *

Opening the door to Gideon's room, Nathan and Abigail saw nothing at first. When they entered the room, however, the lamp in Nathan's hand illuminated the problem. Distraught and bent over, Gideon was holding his ribs, his damp nightshirt hugging his lean frame. Quickly approaching the bed, Nathan set the lamp on the bedside table as Gideon squinted against the light and fell back painfully onto his pillow.

"I am sorry, Nathan. I didn't mean to disturb you," Gideon relayed between labored breaths.

"No need to apologize, son. You just startled us is all," Nathan answered gently.

Her previous misgivings forgotten, Abigail grabbed a cloth from the basin on the table and gently brushed back Gideon's hair with her hand as she wiped the perspiration from his face with the cloth.

Moving to a walnut dresser after that, she retrieved a fresh nightshirt and with her uncle's assistance helped Gideon change. When they noticed his anguish abating, Abigail waited by the edge of the bed while her uncle settled in the chair. Expectant, they watched as Gideon struggled to find words.

"It was a dream," he explained.

Hesitant to share with strangers, he noticed their puzzled faces.

"I am afraid I have them often. They are nightmares really. I guess I get mixed up."

He paused again. It was not easy sharing with these gentle people since they knew nothing of the horrors he had seen.

"Are you feeling better now?" Abigail probed softly, wiping his face again with the cloth.

Beautiful in the lamplight, she distracted him a moment.

"I will be fine," he replied softly as Nathan rose from the chair.

"Well, I think it is time we allow you to get back to sleep, Gideon. If you need anything, just ask.

One of us is sure to hear you," Nathan responded as he prepared another laudanum dose.

When Gideon's benefactors left him, disappearing with the lamp into the hallway, darkness enveloped the room once more. Fighting sleep, he dreaded the nightmare awaiting him, but the laudanum soon took him promptly back to it.

* * *

Pausing in the hallway outside Gideon's room, Abigail gazed up at her uncle as he stopped beside her and lifted the lamp.

"He will be fine," he remarked as the light illuminated her concerned face. After a moment he smiled. "You know, just now in the lamplight, you look just like your mother."

"I do?"

"Yes. Makes me miss her," he shared as they proceeded down the hallway. "Do you know that with all the times I teased her, not once did she tell on me?"

"Not once?" Abigail probed, disbelieving.

"Well, maybe once," he conceded. "She was the dearest sister. Does it ever hurt you, Abigail, being orphaned so young and having to live with an old widower like me?"

Taking his arm, she smiled.

"It is hard to miss what I can barely remember. Besides, I know my mother would have been pleased, knowing you have taken such good care of me. Was she pretty, Uncle Nathan?"

"Pretty?" he echoed, pausing on the stairs landing with her. "Why, just the prettiest girl in the county. I had to fight to keep the courting men away from her, just like I am planning to do for you."

Noting his raised eyebrow, she smiled again. When she glanced back to Gideon's room, her smile faded.

"Will the Yankee be all right, Uncle Nathan?"

"His wounds will heal. But he is hurting pretty bad right now, and I am not referring to what the

Bunch brothers did to him."

Abigail nodded in agreement.

"We did do the right thing then, taking him in, Uncle Nathan?"

"After what we found in his saddlebags? How could we have done anything else?"

She considered her uncle's perspective.

"All right then," she concluded finally. "We best get back to Josiah. He will be wondering what happened up here."

"You know Josiah has feelings for you, Abigail. How do you feel about him?"

"I like him. Any woman would."

"Yes, he could marry any available woman in town, but it is obvious you are the one he wants."

She reflected a moment.

"Josiah is charming, handsome, and a good friend. I do admire him, Uncle Nathan, but more than that, I am not sure."

Regarding her a moment, Nathan glanced down at the lamp as she waited for his response. When he lifted his gaze to her, he smiled.

"You just need to follow your heart, and you will know," he advised softly.

* * *

Waking with a start hours later, Gideon glanced around him apprehensively as moonlight eerily illuminated objects in the room. When he recognized his surroundings as the doctor's house, he breathed a sigh of relief and gingerly moved back against the pillow. Grateful for the moon's soft light, he glanced to the window and reflected on his latest nightmare. Although not as tormenting as some, the dream had left him with a nagging melancholy.

Picturing again the battlefield he had revisited in his dream, he frowned as he recalled the actual memory. He and a steward, Garrett Michaels, had gathered apple butter kettles, filling them with water in a safe location behind the battle lines. Ready with bandages, they had been kept busy after the fighting began, treating the wounded and sending them on to the field hospital. An assistant surgeon at the time, he had always found his work on the battlefield dangerous, but on that particular day, the direction of the fighting changed, putting their aid station in direct line of fire.

After their station was hit, causing wounded and medical staff to scurry, he had attempted to retreat with a wounded soldier as the enemy overran their station. The wounded man next to him fell, however, run through with a bayonet. Right afterward, Gideon received a rifle butt to his forehead, sending him to the ground beside his mortally wounded patient. While a rebel prepared to finish him, Garrett fortunately intervened, knocking the rebel senseless with a tree branch.

With eyes narrowing, Gideon soberly returned to the present as he recalled the dangerous retreat with Garrett back behind enemy lines, sidestepping rebels all the way. Although successful in escaping capture that day, in his dream he and Garrett had not been so fortunate, causing him to wake just as the rebels closed in on them. Returning his gaze to the window, he drew in a breath and sighed. After a while he leaned his head back onto the pillow and closed his eyes, surrendering reluctantly again to sleep.

CHAPTER FIVE

Sitting upright in bed the following afternoon, Gideon found his pain more tolerable and his vision much improved. Having listened to the sounds of town life outside his window all morning from creaking wagons and horse harnesses to a bird's territorial song in the tree outside his window, he tried to picture Braxton Springs, the small town he had yet to see.

"Clara, I am telling you to take this medicine like I told you," Nathan's voice suddenly boomed in a room below Gideon.

"Ya can't tell me what ta do, Doctor Lawrence. I'm not takin' that medicine, I tell ya," Clara protested with equal force.

"You know I am right, Clara. Those old remedies of yours haven't worked. Now take this, or

I will not be helping you any more."

Time seemed suspended as Gideon listened for the woman's reply.

"All right. Give me the poison," she declared in final surrender.

Amused, Gideon tried to envision the cantankerous woman as his bedroom door opened. Spying Abigail in the doorway, her auburn hair pulled back in a stylish snood and her cotton dress replaced with silk, he smiled approvingly.

"Sounds like your uncle is having a time with Clara," he greeted, hoping to engage her in conversation as she approached the bed with a pitcher of water.

With an easy laugh she placed the pitcher on the bedside table.

"Uncle Nathan always does, but Clara still comes back to him. Sort of like some good-natured feud between them, I guess."

She took a step back from him.

"Anything you need? I am going out in just a little while, but I would be glad to get you something before I go. Do you need more laudanum?"

He shook his head.

"I am fine without the laudanum, I think. I would appreciate some company though," he ventured boldly.

Taken off guard a moment, she recovered quickly and retreated to the chair by his bed.

"I take it you are feeling better?" she replied, finding it hard to hide her amusement.

"Yes. And I apologize for disturbing you and your uncle last night. You have both been so kind. I am very grateful."

Receiving his thanks quietly, she thought his eyes seemed bluer for some reason as she slipped gracefully into the chair. Although somewhat self-assured with the measured space between them, her confidence faded when she locked eyes with him, causing her to fidget in the chair.

"I can't sit long. Josiah Peters is picking me up for a buggy ride," she stated, smoothing her skirt nervously.

"Josiah Peters?" Gideon probed, oblivious of

her discomfort.

Abigail nodded.

"Braxton Springs' blacksmith. He has your horse in his stable. When Caleb brought you to our door, Mr. Peters graciously volunteered to see to your horse."

"Has he said how she is doing?"

"He mentioned she is doing very well. It will take some time for her leg to heal, but Mr. Peters is gifted with horses."

Gideon considered this a moment.

"Sounds like a good man. Is he courting you?"

Surprised by his forward manners, Abigail smoothed her skirt again before answering.

"Yes, I guess you could say that."

"I imagine you have any number of single men in Braxton Springs who come calling at your door," he complimented with a smile.

Laughing in spite of his inappropriate remarks, Abigail rose from the chair.

"Mister Taylor, how you do go on. You don't even know me or Josiah Peters or any of the other gentlemen in this town. Do you talk to Northern women this way? They must be charmed beyond belief. I am sure they are just dying for your prompt return," she teased, moving to the door.

"I apologize. I have spoken too directly, haven't I? But I truly meant no offense," he offered sincerely, trying to make up for his error.

Pausing in the doorway, Abigail suppressed a smile as he struggled to think of a way to rectify his social blunder.

"I guess being away at war so long, I have forgotten my manners. I have been in the company of fighting men for over four years, certainly not the most mannerly sort."

"But you, sir, were an officer, were you not?" she teased, finding him charming in spite of his boldness.

"Yes, Miss Lawrence, I was. A major, in fact. You are right, of course. I have no excuse. Would you thank Mr. Peters for me for taking care of my horse?" he responded.

Waiting for her answer, Gideon hoped she

would change her mind and sit again in the chair. Although a foolish notion, he wished it all the same.

"I will be happy to extend your gratitude to Mr. Peters, and rest easy, Major. I assure you, no offense was taken," she replied warmly as she left.

Reflecting on her parting words, he smiled and listened for voices downstairs - her voice and Josiah Peters'.

* * *

Matthew Bunch was irritated. Unsure exactly how to find the Yankee or even Caleb's cabin, his brothers' prattle was getting on his nerves. As he and his brothers tramped through the woods, often dismounting and checking for tracks, the whole search seemed like trying to find the proverbial needle in a haystack. When Seth dismounted again to check the ground for signs, Matthew noted Seth's discouraged sigh.

"Matthew, we ain't never gonna find ole man Caleb's place. Why I herd he don't even live in a normal place," Seth complained.

"Yeah, that's true," Chauncey interjected from atop his horse. "I herd he lives in a cave with some bear."

"Jumpin' Jehoshaphat! We best not mess with a man like that, Matthew. A man who lives with a bear ain't natural," Seth observed.

Dismounting, Matthew angrily approached his brother.

"Lives in a cave, does he? Lives with a bear?" Matthew echoed irritably, pushing Seth back against a tree.

"Well, that's what we herd," Chauncey interrupted timidly.

With contempt Matthew glanced back to Chauncey.

"Well, in that case, when I see the bear, I'm feedin' it the two of you. If it ain't bad enough to have Ma after me, I gotta put up with the two of you as well."

Hurt and confused, Seth and Chauncey fell silent a moment as Matthew released his hold on Seth and returned to his horse.

"Well, what if Caleb took him to town, Matthew?" Chauncey offered hesitantly.

"Ya know as well as I do that Caleb don't cater to no townfolk. He's got him tucked away at his place, I tell ya. Now come on and quit your yappin'," Matthew ordered as he and Seth mounted.

In silence the brothers rode off.

* * *

Standing in the front hallway, Josiah waited expectantly by the front door. Looking quite handsome in his Sunday black coat and pants, he nervously clutched his broad-rimmed hat, his eyes focused on the top of the stairs as Nathan entered the hallway from his office carrying Gideon's saddlebags. When Nathan saw him, he halted momentarily, noting with amusement Josiah's well-groomed appearance.

"Josiah," he greeted, suppressing a smile.

"Good afternoon, Dr. Lawrence. I'm here to take Abigail for a buggy ride."

Nathan nodded.

"Don't be gone too long now, you hear?"

"No, sir. We won't be gone long. How's the Yankee? Will he be leaving any time soon?"

"It will be a while, I expect. He was beaten up pretty bad, but he is faring a lot better," Nathan replied as he ascended the stairs.

Spotting his niece on the landing above him, Nathan paused on the steps and watched her descent.

"Don't be gone long. I heard it might rain," he called after her.

Suppressing a smile, Abigail glanced back to him as she took Josiah's arm and left the house.

CHAPTER SIX

Having heard snatches of the conversation downstairs, Gideon felt frustrated with his recovery rate. More than uneasy being stuck in a Southern town, nice townfolk or not, he impulsively threw back the quilt and determined to get up. Edging off the bed, he braced himself with the bedside table and hesitantly took a step. To his dismay his sprained knee immediately buckled, causing him to lose his balance. He was headed for the floor when Nathan entered the room and ran up alongside him.

"You are not well enough to get up yet, son," Nathan admonished, grabbing onto Gideon's arm as he helped him back into bed. "You need to be patient, Gideon. You will be on your feet soon."

"I don't know what possessed me to do that, Nathan. Impatience, I guess."

Nathan smiled.

"I thought you would be wanting these back, Gideon," he remarked, placing the saddlebags on the bed.

Focusing soberly on the bags a moment, Gideon glanced away to the window. When he returned his gaze to Nathan, he found him seated in the chair quietly watching him.

"Is there something bothering you, son?"

Gideon pensively bit his lip, giving no response.

"Did you ever think it might help to talk about it?"

Gideon glanced down to the quilt. The last thing in the world he wanted to do was talk about it. He had walked away from doctoring for good when he left the hospital in Knoxville, and even though he still had nightmares and became trapped at times in dark memories, he did not relish unveiling them. Nathan thought he was a hero, he was sure, from what he had found in his saddlebags. Why not leave it at that?

"I am not sure I can, Nathan," Gideon replied, avoiding eye contact.

Nathan nodded.

"I am not one to meddle, Gideon, but it seems a might peculiar to me that a man who was given commendations for bravery should act so sheepish about it."

Understanding Nathan's confusion, Gideon nodded.

"It doesn't mean anything, Nathan," he replied, suppressing all emotion as he fingered the quilt absently, hoping to be pressed no further.

"Son, that doesn't make any sense. You are Gideon Taylor, surgeon for the Federal army, right?"

"I was," Gideon replied quietly, his eyes still on the quilt.

"And you were given commendations for bravery, for pulling men off the battlefield in the heat of battle. You pulled them out of the line of fire, Gideon."

Gideon's fingers paused as he reluctantly lifted his gaze.

"It was nothing, Nathan."

"It sounds mighty gallant to me," Nathan countered.

"No, not gallant," Gideon protested with a frown as he dismally anticipated where Nathan was taking him.

"If you are not a hero, what are you then, son?" Nathan probed softly.

Gideon looked away to the window, his eyes narrowing.

"Gideon?" Nathan pressed.

Reluctantly Gideon glanced back to him.

"The medals and commendations were for doing my job, Nathan. Nothing more," he responded. "I was an assistant surgeon at the beginning of the rebellion and spent a lot of time on battlefields. Unfortunately the wounded in this conflict are not just the men with visible wounds and bandages, Nathan. Try as I might, I can't blot out the pain and suffering I have seen or caused on the operating table."

"Seems that the war would be the cause, not

you."

"It is not that simple, Nathan."

"Few things are, Gideon."

With an acknowledging nod, Gideon absently traced the quilt pattern again with his finger while Nathan waited. Finally Gideon's finger stopped.

"My folks died in a freak wagon accident during the war. I grieved something terrible about it. I think now the good Lord meant it as a blessing so they would not have to see how I have changed."

Returning his gaze to the window, Gideon absently focused on the greenery outside as Nathan attentively watched him.

"My mother always said I had a gift for healing, Nathan. Guess it was from all the hurt wild things I would bring home all the time. She said it was preordained by the Almighty. That I could not avoid it. 'My calling,' she said."

Glancing back to Nathan, Gideon flashed him a weak smile as Nathan nodded encouragingly, his eyes fixed on him.

"In response to the rebellion, I went to do my

part with my brother Tom and my best friend, Penrod Yates. We all heard Abraham Lincoln when he spoke in Cincinnati in '59, so when Mr. Lincoln became President and asked for volunteers, we were eager to go. I was fresh out of medical school so was assigned the commission of assistant surgeon."

He paused reflectively.

"We all thought it would be over soon, but it dragged on for years. It was disenchanting for me from the start. Not enough surgeons, a great amount of disorganization at first, terrible living conditions, infernal diseases that would just sweep through a camp, devastating injuries I had never seen before made by the minie ball and cannon, and too many wounded men to treat them properly. It turned out to be much more than I bargained for when I enlisted. Not that I had much time to think about it."

Nathan nodded sympathetically.

"Fortunately my best friend Penn had this way about him that brought out the gentle, even funny things of life even in the midst of the conflict. Penn kept me going."

Realizing the mention of his friend was treading on dangerous territory, Gideon drew in a breath, hoping to extricate himself from the mental quagmire he knew lay ahead if he continued. Noting his discomfort, Nathan moved unobtrusively in his chair and regarded him more intently.

"I got so tired that after a while tired was all I knew, Nathan," Gideon reluctantly continued. "But Penn would stop by my tent and start one of his stories, and it was like a refreshing rain flooding over me somehow, washing away the blood and gore."

Battling stifled emotions, Gideon paused his narrative.

"Penn died at Chattanooga," he finally shared, choking on the words as Nathan leaned forward with concern.

"What happened to him, Gideon?"

"It is not a pretty story," Gideon answered evasively, bottling his emotions once more.

"But maybe it needs to be told," Nathan advised gently.

Hesitant, Gideon bit his lip.

"Penn got wounded on Lookout Mountain, a minie ball shattering his left leg. I had been promoted to operating surgeon by then. The wounded were an unbelievably high number the day they brought him into the field hospital. At the Siege of Chattanooga I never tended so many wounded soldiers as I did those long days and nights. Then they brought in Penn."

Pausing, Gideon futilely resisted as his mind took over, pulling him back to Chattanooga. No longer with Nathan, he found himself in his blood-splattered linen apron, his sleeves rolled up to his elbows. Exhausted and numb, he reached into a basin of crimson water to rinse off his hands as a wounded soldier was placed on the blood-stained table in front of him. Trapped in the familiar nightmare, he cringed when the injured man desperately grabbed his arm.

"Gideon?"

Gideon's tired mind immediately focused.

"Penn, what happened?" he asked, focusing on the shattered leg. Feeling no pulse below the wound, he dismally recognized the need for amputation.

"We were moving across the mountain, Gideon. Place where they sent us at first was all rock above us so they made us move across the mountain. Johnny Reb got me in the leg. I've been waiting the longest time to see you. So many wounded in the fight. So grateful to see your face at last."

Gideon took his friend's hand.

"Penn, listen to me. I have to amputate your leg. It will get infected, and you will die otherwise."

"How will I get to dance with Mary again? She is counting on a dance, Gideon. We promised Mary and her sister, remember?"

"Mary wants you alive, Penn. That is what she wants, not some dance."

While Penn tried to process Gideon's argument, Gideon nodded to his assistant who moved to retrieve the chloroform.

"I won't let you die, Penn. This will save your life. Before you know it, you will be home with Mary, making Tom and me jealous."

"Don't take my leg, Gideon. Please don't take

it," Penn implored weakly as the assistant surgeon turned with funnel in hand.

With eyes widening, Penn grabbed for it, dislodging the funnel from the assistant's grasp. In one swift motion Gideon deftly recovered it, however, positioning the funnel himself over Penn's nose and mouth.

"Penn, I will be here when you wake up. I will help you through this," Gideon promised. "Trust me. This will save your life."

Releasing Penn's hand, Gideon applied the drops of chloroform onto the funnel as the assistant counted aloud Penn's pulse rate. When Penn was asleep, Gideon gave a nod to his assistant to apply the tourniquet while he reached for his knife on the table.

* * *

Moving to the edge of his chair, Nathan watched soberly until Gideon mentally returned, recognizing Nathan at last.

"I amputated Penn's leg. The wound became

septic, and he died a few days later," Gideon reported softly, his eyes on the quilt as he wondered how much of the story he had managed to tell before losing himself at the field hospital.

Genuinely moved, Nathan drew in a breath as Gideon struggled to suppress bottled emotions.

"I have gone over it again and again in my mind, Nathan. I had done so many amputations by then. But sepsis took him in spite of my efforts. I promised I would save his life, but I lost him," he shared softly, his eyes wet.

Nathan nodded soberly.

"Gideon, you did the best you could. You did everything I would have done. It was not your fault. Penn's death was *not* your fault."

Gideon glanced to him.

"But I promised him, Nathan. He trusted me to save his life."

Nathan nodded.

"I know, Gideon, but all we can do as doctors is our best. It sounds like it took a long time before he got to you. The odds were against you, Gideon, to save him at that point."

As Gideon pensively considered Nathan's observation, Nathan rose from the chair.

"You need to let this go, Gideon. I am telling you the truth. His death was not your fault."

Moved by the gracious absolution, Gideon suddenly dissolved under a deluge of suppressed emotions as Nathan anchored on the bed.

"Let it go, Gideon. Let it go," Nathan urged, pulling Gideon to him.

Enveloped in afternoon sunlight, Gideon complied.

CHAPTER SEVEN

When the Bunch brothers finally stumbled onto Caleb's cabin the following morning, they found nothing. Not even Caleb. With no sign of the Yankee about the place, they doggedly returned to their horses to continue their search.

"Looks like maybe I was right, Matthew," Chauncey observed timidly as they mounted. "Maybe Caleb did take 'im to town."

Matthew gave no reply.

"Leastways, we know now Caleb don't live in no cave," Seth stated with relief.

"Yep," Chauncey agreed. "Didn't see no bear around neither."

Matthew rolled his eyes.

"We're headin' into town," Matthew ordered sullenly.

* * *

Seated in the chair that afternoon, Gideon noticed shouting outside his window. Holding an arm to his sore ribs, he braced himself with the bedside table and edged forward to get a better view. When he spied two boys in the yard assaulting a third, he frowned. Unsure how to proceed, he knew for Nathan and Abigail's sake, he needed to remain unseen. Hearing the bedroom door open, he glanced there and spied Nathan. When he beckoned to him, Nathan quickly approached and joined him by the window.

"There is a boy down there who needs your help, I think, Nathan."

Glancing out the window, Nathan spotted the boys.

"Samuel? You and Eugene leave Jed alone. Stop it now and run along home before someone gets hurt," he yelled.

As Samuel and Eugene obeyed, Jed rose slowly to his feet and wiped his nose. Glancing up at the window to Dr. Lawrence, he noticed a stranger next to the doctor who immediately withdrew from sight.

"Jed, are you all right?"

"Yeah, I'm fine, Dr. Lawrence."

"Are you sure? Maybe you should come inside and let me take a look at you."

Jed shook his head.

"I'm fine, Dr. Lawrence. Thanks anyway," Jed replied before running after his friends.

Shaking his head, Nathan turned back to Gideon who had returned to the chair.

"Boys never change. How are you feeling today, Gideon?"

"Much better."

"Glad to hear it, " Nathan responded, perching on the side of the bed across from him.

"Nathan, I am beholding to you for all you have done for me. I know I must put you and your niece in great danger, my being here and all. I just want to assure you that as soon as I am able, I will be on my way. It would grieve me deeply if I caused you any trouble."

Nathan smiled.

"I appreciate that, Gideon, but it has really been no trouble. In fact, I was just wondering this morning if it wasn't Providence that brought you here all along."

Noting Gideon's puzzled expression, Nathan returned to the window and peered down pensively at the yard.

"I am getting up in years, Gideon, and I get right tired. This town will need a doctor when I leave my practice, and it has occurred to me you might be the one to take over for me here."

Gideon's eyes widened.

"Nathan, you can't be serious. Be a doctor in this town? Be a doctor at all after what I told you?"

"What did you tell me, Gideon, that any other doctor wouldn't who has been through the hell of war?"

"Nathan, I took a vow when I left the hospital never to doctor again."

"Why?"

"Because I am not a doctor anymore. I have walked away from all of that."

"Sounds to me like you are trying to run away from it."

Cut by the truth, Gideon frowned.

"Maybe I am, Nathan, but it is all I know how to do."

"That isn't all you know how to do. I bet you are a good surgeon if truth be known."

"No, Nathan. I can't practice medicine anymore. That is just the way it is," Gideon replied, dropping his gaze to his hands.

As silence enveloped the room, Nathan left the window.

"Gideon, how long are you going to serve sentence on yourself for your friend dying?" Nathan probed gently, placing a hand on his shoulder as he drew up beside him. "If you want to hate something, Gideon, hate the war, the terrible conditions, the disease, the infections that robbed you of your patients, but don't hate yourself. There was nothing more you could have done for Penn or any of the other men you lost."

Gideon bit his lip, his eyes fixed on his

hands.

"Your friend Penn sounds like he was a mighty fine man. I know you miss him, Gideon, but Penn would not want you wasting your life because you weren't able to save him. He would want you to go on. Seems to me the best tribute you could give your friend is to save or help as many people as you can, not hide from the world the gift God has given you."

"I took a vow, Nathan, to leave it behind," Gideon insisted, his focus still on his hands.

Allowing quiet to settle on the room again, Nathan leaned in closer.

"Make a new one."

Glancing up sharply, Gideon locked eyes with Nathan.

"I know you are trying to help, Nathan."

"I am just speaking the truth to you, son. No different from what Penn would say if he were here himself. Of that I am certain."

Gideon nodded.

"Yes, Nathan, he probably would," Gideon

conceded reluctantly. "I will think on what you have said. I will give it serious consideration."

"The Lord didn't create the world in a day. Takes time, Gideon."

Hearing someone entering the house downstairs, Nathan retreated to the bedroom door.

"You are wrong, you know," Nathan concluded, glancing back to him from the doorway. "Your mother was right. It *is* your calling, Gideon."

* * *

Soon after Nathan's departure, Gideon heard someone in the doorway. Glancing there, he spied Abigail approaching with a bouquet of flowers.

"Miss Lawrence," he greeted, his spirits lifting considerably.

"Good afternoon, Major," she replied, placing the wildflowers in the water pitcher on his bedside table. "I picked these today for you during my afternoon walk with my friend Amelia."

Gideon's eyes widened.

"For me?" he asked, eyeing the flowers.

"Yes, I thought after all you have been through, these flowers might cheer you up a bit."

"They do, Miss Lawrence, much more than you know," he confirmed with a smile.

"Well, I need to start supper so I best be going," she concluded, heading back toward the door.

"Miss Lawrence?"

Pausing, she turned to him.

"Did Mr. Peters happen to mention how my horse is doing?"

With a nod she took a few steps toward him.

"He said he is keeping your mare still in the stall so her leg can heal. He thinks she will be fine. He is coming here for supper tonight so you can talk with him yourself if you like."

Pleased with her report, he glanced again to the flowers.

"Where did you say you found these beautiful flowers? I have never seen any like these in Cincinnati."

"Is that where you are from, Major?" she

answered, advancing as far as the chair.

"Yes, Miss Lawrence. My family owns a farm a few miles west of Cincinnati. My brother Tom and I grew up there. We ran all over the countryside as boys but never saw flowers like these."

"So you ended up in Tennessee because of the war, Major?"

Gideon's smile faded.

"Yes, Miss Lawrence. I have served on battlefields and in hospitals all over the state of Tennessee. I finished my service at a hospital in Knoxville, in fact. I was late starting home because I had to help clear the hospital there after the war ended."

"I see. So you have probably seen more of my state than I have, Major. Do you have a medical practice waiting for you when you get back to Cincinnati?"

Gideon shook his head.

"I am going to help my brother with the family farm. Our folks died this past year in a wagon accident so Tom needs my help. He is already there, having mustered out of the infantry last September."

"But won't you miss doctoring, Major? I can't imagine Uncle Nathan doing anything else."

Gideon frowned.

"I am trying to put it behind me, Miss Lawrence," he confessed soberly, dropping his gaze to his hands.

Her eyes narrowed.

"I apologize, Major. I didn't realize it was a painful topic for you," she replied, taking another step closer.

"Actually, Miss Lawrence, I am finding it harder to walk away from than I thought."

"Is the war the source of your nightmares?" she probed gently, stopping next to the bed.

Gideon swallowed hard.

"Yes, Miss Lawrence. As I said before, I am sorry for the other night."

"No need to apologize, Major. I think it is a fine thing you did, helping wounded men during the long conflict no matter what color uniform they wore."

He flashed her a weak smile.

"Well, enjoy your flowers while I go fix supper. We will talk again later," she promised, issuing him a warm smile.

When she reached the doorway, she paused and glanced back to him.

"The name of the wildflower is Passion Flower. I heard it only grows in Tennessee," she added as she left him.

Gideon glanced again to the flowers.

"Passion Flower," he repeated softly, eyeing the purple blooms with a smile.

CHAPTER EIGHT

"Supper was delicious, Abigail, but I do believe the spoon bread was my favorite," Josiah complimented from the kitchen table as he watched her working at the dry sink.

"Thank you, Josiah," she answered, turning back to the table to retrieve another plate.

To her surprise he stayed her hand.

"Abigail, I think you know I have feelings for you, and I've been hoping you have similar sentiments for me."

"Josiah, I do think highly of you."

"You do?"

"Yes," she assured him, moving back to the sink with the plate.

Leaving the table, Josiah drew up beside her. After a few minutes she glanced to him and smiled.

"Did you know the soldier Caleb brought us

earned commendations for bravery for saving men on the battlefield?"

His face clouded.

"What did you bring him up for?"

Turning to face him, Abigail wiped her hands on her apron.

"I just thought you might feel better if you knew he was a hero."

"I don't really care what he has done," he answered, finding it hard to hide his resentment. "If it weren't for my cousin Ike fighting for the Union, I may not have even helped him, taking his horse and all."

"Really? Do you mean that?"

"Yes, I do. Ike has always been my favorite cousin. When Caleb brought the Yankee here, all I could think of was Ike and if someone would've helped him in a similar situation."

"Well, I think you did the right thing. I didn't at first, but I do now."

"Yes, I can see that," he answered irritably.

Hearing the back door fly open, the startled

pair glanced there.

"Bunch brothers been here?" Caleb greeted gruffly from the open doorway.

"N-no. Why?" Abigail answered, finding her voice at last.

"I tracked 'em here. They were at ma cabin. I assume they're after the Yankee. Is he still here?"

"Yes. He is upstairs. Uncle Nathan just took supper up to him," she reported.

As Caleb headed for the house stairs, Abigail and Josiah exchanged glances.

"This can't be good, Josiah. Do you think Caleb is right? Are the Bunches looking for him?"

"Considering he's a Yankee, Abigail, I think they could be. Remember what happened to their brother Abel in the war?"

"But the major is a doctor, Josiah. There is no way he could have killed Abel. He saved men's lives."

"I doubt that means much to the Bunches, Abigail."

* * *

"Doc?" Caleb bellowed from the bedroom doorway, startling Nathan by the window.

Equally surprised, Gideon looked up from his supper in the chair.

"Caleb, what is it?" Nathan asked, puzzled by the visit.

"Bunch brothers. Tracked 'em to town. They already been ta my place, messin' up my cabin like they were searchin' fer somethin'. No doubt it's you," Caleb warned, glancing to Gideon.

Forgetting his supper, Gideon soberly absorbed the ominous report.

"Is Josiah still downstairs, Caleb?" Nathan asked, joining him in the doorway.

"Was a few minutes ago."

Nathan glanced back to Gideon.

"Don't give it another thought, Gideon. We will handle this."

Gideon began to respond, but Nathan left.

"You are the man who saved my life," Gideon observed, turning his attention to Caleb.

Caleb regarded him indifferently.

"I am obliged to you although frankly I don't remember much," Gideon continued.

"Don't reckon ya would. The Bunch brothers had beat ya almost senseless."

"You live in the mountains, Dr. Lawrence told me," Gideon reported, focusing a moment on Caleb's buckskins which seemed more attuned to the Wild West than the rural South.

"Yeah. Can't stand it here for too long. Too cramped and people too bothersome. Leastways, most of 'em."

Appreciating Caleb's sentiment, Gideon had also learned the comfort solitude afforded during rare, quiet moments away from the field hospitals during the war.

"The Bunch brothers. Who are they?" Gideon probed.

"Pack of cowardly skunks. They gang up on someone like you, alone and defenseless, but scurry like rats if they have to fight fair. Ya best lie low till they're gone."

"You think then they are still after me?"

"They come ta town 'bout as often as me. Ya kin bet they ain't here to inspect the latest yard goods at the mercantile."

Gideon frowned.

* * *

When Nathan returned to the kitchen, Abigail and Josiah paused their conversation.

"Josiah, you best get to the stable. If the Bunch brothers find his horse there, we will be in a fix for sure," Nathan directed before retreating down the hall to his office.

"I should check on Gideon," Abigail mused aloud, moving to follow her uncle.

Unhappy with the familiar reference, Josiah frowned, resenting Gideon even more.

"I don't know but that it might be a good idea for the Bunch brothers to take him," Josiah openly declared, causing Abigail to turn to him.

"Josiah Peters, you don't mean that. How could you say such a thing?"

"Oh, it's not hard," he answered coldly as

Caleb passed through the kitchen and left the house without a word.

"What do you mean, Josiah?"

"I mean he doesn't belong here, Abigail. He's a Yankee, remember?" Sensing her disappointment in him, he turned and exited the house.

"Josiah?" she called from the back doorway, causing Caleb to glance to her from the yard as he left with his mule.

Josiah did not look back.

* * *

When Josiah reached the livery, he heard voices inside the stable. Assuming the Bunch brothers were inside, he moved into the darkness at the corner of the building and eyed the stable's open doorway. Feeling tempted to inform the brothers of Gideon's location, he dropped his gaze to his boots and resolved to do it, justifying such an action as his duty until he pondered Abigail's reaction.

She obviously cared more for the Yankee

than she would admit. On the other hand, if he turned Gideon over to the Bunches, she might understand in time. Anguishing over his indecision, he shook his head and left the corner of the livery.

* * *

A sound came from the front hallway. Protectively placing Abigail behind him, Nathan left his office to investigate. To his surprise he spied Gideon descending the last steps of the stairs toting his coat and saddlebags. Dressed in his own clothes, he seemed equally startled to see Nathan. Then his injured knee buckled, and he started to fall. Nathan quickly grabbed onto him, keeping him upright as Abigail also lended support.

"Thanks," Gideon responded, putting his full weight on his healthy leg.

"Gideon, what are you doing, son? Get back to bed," Nathan urged.

"No, Nathan, this is my fight. Not yours. The last thing I would want is to put your lives in danger."

"Nothing is going to happen to us if you just get back upstairs where you belong," Nathan argued, steering Gideon back to the stairs.

Pulling away, Gideon braced himself with the stairs' newel post.

"My mind is made up, Nathan. The Bunch brothers will not bother you if I am not here."

Noting Nathan's frown, Gideon glanced to Abigail.

"Would you help me with my coat, Miss Lawrence?"

With reluctance she complied.

Issuing her a grateful smile, Gideon retrieved his saddlebags and hobbled toward the front door.

Nathan shook his head.

"Gideon, have you lost your mind?" he protested, observing his awkward gait.

"What do you mean, Nathan?"

"Where are you planning to go? And just how are you going to get there? You are in no condition to go anywhere yet."

"I will manage somehow. Maybe I can hide at the livery."

"No, Major. Don't go there. Promise me," Abigail implored, recalling Josiah's angry exit.

Moved by her concern, he smiled.

"I mean it, Major. Don't go there," she insisted.

"All right," he answered softly.

"Wait here a minute," Nathan ordered, retreating into his office.

Confused by the request, Gideon reluctantly obliged. When Nathan returned with a cane, his face brightened.

"Thank you, Nathan. That will help a great deal," he responded, taking the cane from him.

"You need to go out the back, Gideon," Nathan instructed, taking his arm.

Appreciating Nathan and Abigail's assistance, Gideon hobbled down the hallway into the kitchen. When they reached the back door, he paused.

"Thanks for everything, Nathan," he stated earnestly, gripping the doctor's hand. "I can never repay you for your kindness."

"I wish you would reconsider, son. You are not strong enough to go anywhere. You couldn't have made it this far without help."

"Perhaps if I went with you, Major, I could lend support and show you the way," Abigail offered.

"I appreciate the offer, Miss Lawrence, but it is best you don't know where I am. I will never forget what you have done for me though."

Boldly taking her hands, he regarded her one last time, noting the concern in her hazel eyes as he resisted the temptation to stay. Reluctantly he released her.

"I best be going," he concluded, exiting the house as dusk's protective cover spread across the Lawrence property.

"Gideon?" Nathan called from the doorway.

Pausing in the yard, Gideon glanced back to him.

"Gideon, come back, son. We can hide you till the Bunches leave town. Your setting out on your own like this is foolhardy."

Gideon shook his head.

"I will be fine, Nathan. Hope to see you both again some day. Thanks again," he responded before disappearing around the corner of the house.

With a sigh Nathan retreated back inside with Abigail and closed the back door.

"How will he ever manage, Uncle Nathan?" she asked plaintively.

"Gideon is in God's hands now, Abigail," he replied, wrapping an arm around her as they left the kitchen together. When they were almost to the parlor, the front door flew open before them.

"Dr. Lawrence?" Josiah greeted, panting in the open doorway.

"What is it, son?" Nathan probed.

"Not good news, I'm afraid. But I thought you should know."

"Know what?" Abigail asked, her mind racing.

"The Bunch brothers have been to the stable. I don't know how they could've missed the Yankee's horse."

Abigail drew in a breath.

"What do you plan to do?" Josiah pressed.

"It is already done," Nathan replied wistfully.

"What do you mean?" Josiah questioned, noting Abigail's equally sad expression.

"Gideon is gone," Nathan explained.

Josiah's eyes widened.

"Gone?" he echoed, his face brightening. "Then there's nothing to fear. We can just get on with our lives."

Nathan and Abigail frowned.

"What made him leave?" he asked, oblivious of the pair's disappointment in him.

"He was afraid for us," Abigail responded.

Josiah considered this a moment.

"It was good of you to come and tell us, Josiah," Nathan remarked before turning to his niece. "I am going upstairs, Abigail, to see if Gideon left anything."

Nodding absently, she dismally pictured Gideon outside in the dark with the Bunch brothers. With a sigh she turned to Josiah.

"I am surprised you came back, Josiah."

Josiah bit his lip.

"I'm sorry, Abigail. I said some things that weren't very proper. Believe me, when I thought the Bunch brothers were in the livery, I felt tempted to turn the Yankee over to them. Then I realized I couldn't really do that."

Getting no response, he shifted his weight uncomfortably.

"I was jealous, Abigail. Jealous of the time you spent with him and how you talked of him being a hero so enchanted like. I beg your pardon for acting the way I did."

She flashed him a weak smile.

"You are a fine man, Josiah Peters."

CHAPTER NINE

Loitering outside the mercantile, the Bunch brothers noted the lamps being lit in town windows as darkness settled on Braxton Springs. Unsure how to proceed, Matthew pondered their next move as Jed and his friend Eugene came tearing around the corner of the general store and ran straight into Seth.

"Where ya goin', ya little varmit?" Seth threatened, grabbing Jed's arm.

Swallowing hard, Jed wriggled to get loose until Matthew seized him by the hair. As the boy quickly gave up the struggle, his friend Eugene bravely started a protest. After hearing Matthew's responsive growl, however, Eugene promptly scurried off toward home, abandoning Jed to the notorious brothers.

Matthew held up a lantern to Jed's face.

"Ya seen a Yankee anywheres in town?" Matthew bellowed.

Drawing in an anxious breath, Jed shook his head as he regarded the brothers' sullen faces and struggled to think, hoping to come up with something to earn his release. When he remembered the stranger in Dr. Lawrence's window, his eyes brightened.

"Only stranger I seen in town was the one at Doc Lawrence's place. But he didn't have on no Yankee uniform that I saw," Jed offered.

"Doc's place?" Matthew echoed.

"Yeah, I saw him at Doc's."

"Should a knowed. Come on," Matthew ordered his brothers.

Releasing Jed with a forceful shove, Seth retreated down the street with Matthew and Chauncey as Jed hurried off in the opposite direction to find a good hiding place.

* * *

Dropping Red's saddle at his feet, Gideon

hugged his aching ribs and grimaced. The journey to the livery had taken almost all of his endurance, and now his ribs' painful protest was preventing his escape.

"We need to get out of here, Red, if I could just mount you somehow."

As he glanced around the dimly lit stable for a stool or bucket, he heard footsteps in the stable doorway. Catching a glimpse of a glowing lantern, he crouched down next to his mare.

"Who's there? You better show yourself, or I'll shoot," Josiah called from the open doorway.

Getting no response, Josiah hung his lantern on the barn post and moved into the tack room for a rifle. Emerging moments later with the gun, he noticed rustling back by the Yankee's horse.

"I said I'll shoot. Show yourself," Josiah threatened, moving warily toward Red's stall.

Painfully complying, Gideon rose, revealing himself.

"You?" Josiah declared with surprise.

Retrieving the lantern, Josiah held it up,

illuminating his rival and the saddle at his feet.

"You just fixin' to ride out of here?" Josiah asked, stifling a smile.

Gideon remained silent.

"You wouldn't get to the end of the street before you'd be flat on your face on the ground," Josiah remarked.

Gideon smiled weakly.

"And your horse isn't ready to be ridden yet, anyway," Josiah reported, becoming serious.

"Unfortunately there are some men here in town who would like to finish what they started with me outside of town so I do not stand a chance if I wait around here."

Josiah nodded.

"I would say your chances are a might slim."

"Are you Josiah Peters?"

"Yeah, I'm the blacksmith here in town. And you're Gideon Taylor. I was at the Lawrences' when Caleb deposited you on their back porch. You kind of interrupted our supper, Gideon," he teased, finding his resentment for him quickly abating.

"I apologize for that," Gideon replied, flashing him a weak smile. "How is Red?" he asked, stroking his mare's nose.

"She'll be fine, but you can't ride her yet."

"I guess then I am in a predicament here."

With a confirming nod Josiah watched with interest as Gideon took a step backward and supported himself with the stable wall.

"I appreciate your taking care of my horse. Red and I have been through a lot together."

Josiah nodded an acknowledgment.

Battling weariness, Gideon glanced down to the stable floor, trying to muster strength.

Josiah bit his lip.

"You better lie down before you keel over on me. C'mon," Josiah directed, helping Gideon into the tack room.

Clearing bridles away with his arm, Josiah eased Gideon down onto a wooden bed.

"Why don't you rest yourself awhile? The Bunch brothers have already been here. I doubt they will come back any time soon."

Nodding appreciatively, Gideon closed his eyes as Josiah retreated into the stable to fetch a canteen. Minutes later he returned.

"Thirsty?" Josiah asked.

With a grateful nod Gideon took the offered canteen and drank. Leaning back afterward against the wall, he eyed his caretaker.

"I guess I was right about you, Josiah."

Josiah's eyes narrowed.

"What do you mean?"

"I told Miss Lawrence you are a good man."

"You talked about me with Miss Lawrence?"

"Yes. She is very special, Josiah, like an angel of mercy," Gideon averred, taking another drink.

Feeling jealousy flare, Josiah let it pass as he lifted Gideon's injured leg up onto the bed and noted his discomfort. Regarding him a moment, he begrudgingly could see why Abigail liked him. With a sigh he began hanging up the strewn bridles on the tack room wall.

* * *

Congregated with his brothers on the Lawrence porch, Matthew pounded on the front door. When Nathan opened it, Matthew noticed the lamp in Nathan's hand and stepped boldly into the light.

"What brings you here so late, Matthew? Someone sick out at your place?" Nathan asked.

"Nope, Doc," Seth interjected, stepping into the light with Chauncey. "Ma and Martha are jest fine."

"We want the Yankee," Matthew reported, moving past Nathan into the house as his brothers followed.

"Now what would you want with a Yankee?" Nathan asked.

"This ain't no social call, Doc," Matthew protested, glancing into the parlor. "We want him now."

"But he isn't here."

Matthew frowned.

"We don't mean ya no harm, Doc, but if ya git in the way, that'll be yore probl'm. All we want is the Yankee, and we know he's here. The boy down the street told us he'd seen 'im here," Matthew reported.

Hearing the brothers' arrival, Abigail left the kitchen. Visibly overcome by her presence, the brothers moved uncomfortably when she stopped near them.

"I was wondering what all the commotion was about. Are Martha and your mother all right?" she asked, wiping her hands on her apron.

Dumbstruck, Seth and Chauncey flashed her timid smiles.

"We've come fer the Yankee. Boy in town said he'd seen the Yank here at yore house," Matthew explained, noticeably subdued.

"Well, yes, he was here, but that was awhile ago. Caleb brought him here, but he is long gone by now. Didn't my uncle tell you that?" she replied, glancing to her uncle.

"I was trying to tell them that, Abigail, but I don't think they have heard a word I have said," Nathan responded.

"Matthew Bunch," she continued sweetly, "you don't think we would keep a Yankee here for very long, do you?"

"But a boy down the street said he was here," Matthew countered, his face puzzled.

"Well, if you feel a need to search the place and disrupt our evening, go ahead, but I would take it as an intrusion personally," she remarked.

 Matthew pensively bit his lip.

"When did he leave, Doc?" he asked, his voice less strident now.

"A day ago."

"Ya didn't see which way he was headed?" he pressed.

"North. He was headed home, I think."

Matthew turned to his brothers.

"Come on."

Nodding to Abigail as they passed her, Seth and Chauncey followed Matthew out of the house. Promptly closing the door behind them, Nathan turned back to her and sighed.

CHAPTER TEN

Standing in the tack room doorway, Josiah regarded his rival pensively.

"I've been thinking it over, and the way I see it, the Bunch brothers won't be comin' back here so you'd be safe just to stay here for a while. You're in no condition to ride, Gideon."

"I appreciate the offer," Gideon replied, rubbing his injured leg.

"Pain pretty bad?"

Gideon nodded.

Walking over to some hanging bridles, Josiah reached behind them and pulled out a flask.

"I keep it in case of emergencies, if you know what I mean," he explained, handing it to Gideon with a smile.

Returning Josiah's smile, Gideon nodded and

took a swig. Although the whiskey burned all the way down, he took another drink before glancing to his caretaker.

"Why are you doing this for me, Josiah?"

"I'm not. It's for Abigail. She would never forgive me if I let something happen to you and could have stopped it. Believe me, I'm no Yankee sympathizer although you'll find divided loyalties among the townspeople in Braxton Springs."

Absorbed in the revelation that Abigail would be concerned about him, Gideon gave no response.

"Had a cousin Ike who fought for the Union. Don't know for sure if he survived the war or not," Josiah continued.

"What was his name?" Gideon asked dully, the alcohol enveloping his senses.

"Peters, like mine. You know him?"

Shaking his head, Gideon eased back against the wall, lightheaded all of a sudden. When Josiah offered him a blanket, he took it gratefully, pulling it up around him as the liquor spread through his system. Surrendering to the welcome numbness,

Gideon closed his eyes while Josiah finished hanging bridles.

* * *

The Bunch brothers had not gotten more than thirty yards down the street when Matthew stopped abruptly and raised his arm, causing his brothers to halt. As Seth and Chauncey regarded him quizzically, Matthew glanced back to the Lawrence house.

"Somethin's not right about this. Somethin' jest don't smell right," Matthew declared.

Seth sniffed the air.

"What do ya mean, Matthew? I don't smell nothin'."

Flashing Seth a scornful glance, Matthew strode back down the street while Seth and Chauncey meekly followed. When the trio reached the Lawrences' front porch, Matthew bounded up the steps and pounded forcefully on the door.

* * *

Josiah had just hung up the last of the bridles in the tack room when he heard a rustling out in the stable. Exiting the tack room, he grabbed a lantern off the post and advanced toward the sound.

"Who's there?" he called, waving his lantern into empty stalls until he discovered Jed crouched in a stall corner. "What in the blazes are you doin' there, boy? Come out of there."

When Jed obeyed, Josiah guided the boy toward the stable door. To his surprise, the boy suddenly pulled away.

"Look, Jed, I don't know what trouble you're in this time, but I don't have time for this tonight. You run home to your ma and pa. It's well past dark. They're probably worried sick."

"No, Josiah, I can't."

"Jedediah Coulter, what do you mean? You best stop with this nonsense and get home," he insisted, leading him again toward the door.

"Not till the Bunch brothers leave town, Josiah," Jed responded, pulling away from him again.

Josiah's eyes narrowed.

"What are you talkin' about? Did you see them?"

"They made me tell about the stranger I seen lookin' out Doc Lawrence's window."

"What stranger?"

"The one I seen peekin' through the upstairs window when Doc was hollerin' at Samuel and Eugene."

"You told the Bunch brothers you saw him?"

Jed nodded.

Josiah stifled alarm.

"And they threatened they was comin' fer me if they didn't find 'im. I was too scared ta go home, Josiah."

Placing a comforting hand on the boy's shoulder, Josiah heard a sound behind him. Turning responsively with Jed, he spied Gideon in the tack room doorway.

Jed's eyes widened.

"Yore him," the boy cried with alarm. "Josiah, he's the man I seen at the window. Now I know I'm good as dead. He's not at the doc's, and the

Bunches will come fer me fer sure."

"What is it? What is the boy saying?" Gideon probed, leaning against the door frame for support.

"Seems like Jed saw you at the Lawrences' one day when he was playing with his friends. He has told the Bunch brothers."

"The Lawrences need to be warned, Josiah," Gideon responded with a frown.

Nodding in agreement, Josiah promptly guided the boy over to Gideon.

"You take care of the boy, Gideon. I'll go warn the Lawrences. I should be back soon," he promised, retrieving his rifle.

After Josiah's departure Gideon glanced down to the boy. Obviously uncomfortable in Gideon's presence, Jed reluctantly retreated with him into the tack room.

* * *

Bounding down the Lawrence house stairs, Seth and Chauncey joined Matthew and the

Lawrences in the front hallway.

"Nobody up there, Matthew," Seth reported.

"Not a trace of 'im anywheres," Chauncey confirmed.

"Where ya got him hid, Doc?"

"I told you, Matthew. He is gone."

"Do ya think I'm stupid, Doc?" Matthew challenged.

Biting his lip, Nathan gave no reply.

"We near beat the Yank to death so there's no way he could a left here a day ago. And do ya think he'd leave without his horse?" Matthew asked scornfully. "Chauncey, you two tear this place apart if ya have ta. He's gotta be here somewhere."

"Now hold on there," Nathan protested. "Matthew, I cannot figure out for the life of me why you are so dead set on killing the man. He is a doctor, you know. He never even fought in the war. He worked in Union hospitals. He couldn't have shot your brother Abel. He received commendations for saving men's lives."

Matthew frowned.

"His bein' a doctor don't make no difference ta me. I said before, Doc, I didn' want to hurt ya none, but if ya know what's good fer ya, you'll be tellin' me where he's at and save us all a heap of trouble," Matthew threatened.

Hearing the front door open, Matthew and his brothers glanced there expectantly. With dismay they spied Josiah.

"Havin' a bit of trouble here, Doctor Lawrence?" Josiah greeted, training his rifle on the brothers. "I heard the commotion clear outside. Figured you and Miss Lawrence might need some help."

"I am obliged, Josiah," Nathan answered.

"I think it's best you all leave, Matthew," Josiah advised, cocking his rifle.

Matthew reluctantly nodded to Seth and Chauncey who obediently left the house with him.

"Matthew?" Nathan called from the front doorway.

Pausing on the porch step, Matthew glanced back to him.

"I told you he isn't here, and it is the truth. He is a doctor, like I said. Why don't you just let this go, Matthew?"

"Nope. We're gonna find 'im, Doc. Ya can count on it."

With a sigh Nathan shook his head and retreated back inside the house as Josiah lowered his rifle and closed the door.

"You could not have picked a better time to come calling, Josiah," Nathan offered gratefully as Abigail nodded in agreement.

"I didn't come calling, Nathan. I was warned."

* * *

Sitting at the far end of the tack room bed, Jed eyed his caretaker closely. Gideon had his eyes closed and was leaning back against the tack room wall at the opposite end of the bed so Jed felt free to gawk.

"So yore a real Yankee?"

Gideon opened his eyes.

"I am real all right."

"I don't get it."

"Get what?"

"Why are the Doc and Josiah hidin' ya out?"

Running a hand back through his hair, Gideon eyed the boy wearily.

"Maybe because the war is over."

"That don't make no difference, mister," Jed fired back.

"Seems to be the general opinion around here."

"Well, it don't. I probably did the right thing tellin' 'em about ya."

Frowning at the boy's prejudice, Gideon leaned back against the wall and closed his eyes, yielding again to the alcohol.

"How many men did ya kill, Yank?"

"Far too many to count," Gideon answered, his eyes still closed.

Scooting apprehensively to the very end of the bed, Jed eyed him with more respect.

"What's it like killin' somebody?" Jed asked timidly.

"It is a very terrible thing," Gideon answered, opening his eyes as he heard someone entering the stable.

While he scanned the room for a rifle, Jed ran for the door. Exiting the tack room, Jed ran straight into Matthew Bunch.

"Oh, God," the boy exclaimed as Matthew grabbed his arm.

"Yore a plumb fool, boy, if ya think God will be helpin' ya. So yore why the blacksmith showed his face at the Doc's. I think it's time, boy, ya wuz taught a lesson. Fetch a whip, Seth."

As Seth obeyed, Chauncey tied Jed to a stable post. Seizing the whip from Seth's hands, Matthew sullenly turned to the terrified boy.

"This is one lesson yore never gonna forgit, boy, if ya live to tell about it," Matthew threatened, raising the whip in his hand.

"Put the whip down."

Surprised, the brothers glanced behind them and spied Gideon braced against the tack room door frame with a rifle leveled their direction. Seth and

Chauncey promptly exchanged fearful glances. Matthew, on the other hand, could see Gideon was not that strong, having to support himself with the door frame. Still, he eyed the gun with respect.

"Let the boy go," Gideon ordered.

Sullenly Matthew glanced to his brothers and nodded. Once free, Jed quickly left his captors and joined Gideon, his face registering a new, reverent respect for the Yankee.

"I was wonderin', Yank, if we were gonna have to tear this whole town apart lookin' fer ya. It's nice ya saved us the trouble," Matthew taunted.

Ignoring Matthew, Gideon glanced down to Jed.

"Go get Josiah at the Lawrence house. I will hold them here. Run as fast as you can."

With a nod Jed left the stable on a run.

"What ya fixin' to do, Yank? Shoot us all down?" Matthew challenged as Seth and Chauncey's eyes widened at the prospect.

Fighting a wave of weakness, Gideon gave no response, emboldening the brothers in spite of his rifle. Like predatory vultures awaiting dinner, they watched his movements, waiting for the opportunity to strike.

"What is your pressing need to track me down? Didn't you get your fill back at the stream?" Gideon protested.

"No, Yank, that was jest a taste," Matthew responded, his eyes fixed on him.

When Gideon shifted his weight, his gun pointed down momentarily so the vultures swooped in, overpowering him easily as they knocked him backward onto the tack room floor. Before he could rise, Seth and Chauncey grabbed his arms and hauled him up before Matthew.

"Tie him to your saddle, Seth, and ride behind him back home. Let's git before that boy comes back with the whole town," Matthew ordered.

With eager nods, Seth and Chauncey followed Matthew out of the stable, their captive in tow.

CHAPTER ELEVEN

Bounding up the Lawrence porch steps, Jed pounded on the front door and anxiously waited until the door opened.

"What is it, Jed?" Nathan greeted.

"It's the Bunch brothers. The Yankee's holdin' a gun on 'em at the stable, and he asked me to get Josiah."

Hearing his name, Josiah joined Nathan in the doorway along with Abigail.

"He saved me, Josiah," Jed reported. "The Bunch brothers was gonna whip me, but the Yankee risked his life fer me. He seems awful weak though. Ya need ta come fast. I don't know how long he can hold 'em there by himself."

With a nod Josiah stepped out onto the porch as the Bunches rode past on their horses.

"They've got the Yankee," Jed cried with alarm.

"Jed?" a man's voice interjected.

Glancing away from the others, Jed saw his father approaching the porch.

"Pa, they were gonna whip me, and the Yankee saved me. He could a stayed hid, but he helped me instead. And now they've got 'im, Pa," the boy cried plaintively, running into his father's arms.

"What are you talkin' about, Jed? Eugene said you were in trouble with the Bunch brothers. I've been lookin' all over fer ya," Tom Coulter replied, squatting down to his son's level.

"They had a whip, Pa, and were plannin' on beatin' me. They would've too if the Yankee hadn't stepped in."

Thunder sounded.

"Come inside a moment, Tom. Bring Jed," Nathan encouraged.

As Tom complied, Abigail turned to Josiah whose focus was on the end of the street where he had last seen the Bunches.

"Josiah, if you do not go after them, they will kill him for sure. They were so angry here tonight. I cannot imagine what they will do to him now that they have him," she stated plaintively.

"Josiah?" Tom interrupted, returning quickly to the porch. "I'll git my brother Ned, and we'll ride with ya to the Bunches if that will help. Sounds like this man saved ma son tonight."

"Yes, Tom, he did," Josiah confirmed with a nod.

* * *

Smoking her pipe in her rocker by the fire, Sarah eyed the unconscious Yankee lying in the corner of the cabin. She had been pleased when her sons had brought him, giving the men some peace. Now they just awaited her decree on the Yankee's future.

Keeping guard over their captive with his rifle, Seth glanced a moment at the rain pelting the windows before regarding his charge again. The Yankee had not moved since they dragged him inside. He had passed out during the ride to the cabin, but Seth had followed Matthew's orders and tied him to the saddle, keeping him securely atop the horse.

Seated near her mother by the hearth, Martha regarded the stranger with interest. She thought him handsome so she found it hard to believe her mother would do him any serious harm in spite of her mother's vow for vengeance on all Yankees after Abel's death in the war. With widening eyes Martha saw the stranger stir.

Noting the movement as well, Sarah promptly put down her pipe and strode to him, picking up a lamp from the table on her way. As a loud clap of thunder sounded, she held the lamp to Gideon's face as he stirred again and squinted up against the light.

"Don't move, Yank," Seth warned, cocking the rifle.

"Nobody followed ya home?" Sarah asked, glancing back to Matthew and Chauncey eating at the table.

"No one, Ma. Prob'ly the rain," Matthew

answered between bites. "We kept a close lookout all the way."

"Who'd help a Yankee anyway, Ma?" Chauncey interjected, glancing up from his stew.

Appalled at the squalor of the place, Gideon glanced around him, noting the young girl staring from the hearth. When he returned his gaze to Sarah, he squinted again against the lamplight.

"Ma'am?"

"Don't ya make no appeal to me, Yank. There's only one thing ta do with ya before those meddlin' townfolk show their faces here. Kill 'im," Sarah ordered coldly.

Shocked at the death sentence, Gideon drew in a breath as Sarah returned to her rocker to wait for her justice to be carried out. The only sympathetic person in the room seemed to be the young girl by the fire who seemed as equally disturbed as Gideon that her brothers were about to kill him right before her eyes.

When Seth glanced back to Matthew for a signal, Gideon realized it was his only chance.

Mustering all of his strength, he made a rush for the gun. Surprised by the move, Seth struggled with him while Matthew and Chauncey left the table to help. Suddenly the rifle fired, followed by a scream from the hearth.

Forgetting the struggle momentarily, the men glanced across the cabin to Sarah kneeling by Martha near the fire. Angry now, Seth sent Gideon sprawling back into the corner with a blow from the rifle butt and quickly trained his gun on him again before glancing back apprehensively to his sister as Chauncey cleared a place for her on the table with a sweep of his arm against the plates. When Matthew placed Martha's limp form atop the pine boards, Sarah drew up anxiously beside her.

"It looks bad," she reported after examining the wound. "She needs Doc Lawrence."

"I'll go right away, Ma," Chauncey offered.

"Wait," Matthew interjected, grabbing his brother's sleeve. "Ma, Doc Lawrence tole me the Yank here wasn't a regular soldier. He was a doc in the war. He worked in Yankee hospitals. He can tend to

Martha."

"Is that true, Yank?" Sarah barked, her eyes narrowing.

Gideon gave no reply.

Advancing menacingly to Gideon, Matthew jerked him up onto his feet.

"Did Doc Lawrence tell me the truth?" he bellowed.

"If ya want to live a while longer, Yank, ya best be tellin' us. Are ya a doctor or not?" Sarah snarled, drawing up next to him.

Gideon felt caught in a nightmare.

"I was during the war but not anymore."

Not liking Gideon's answer, Matthew pinned him against the wall.

"Ya know doctorin?" he yelled.

"Yes," Gideon reluctantly replied.

"Ya best save my Martha's life then. Ya save her, Yank, or yore a dead man," Sarah threatened as Matthew dragged Gideon to the table.

Glancing down to the girl as the family gathered around him, Gideon mechanically checked her wound and vital signs while the Bunches critically watched his movements. In spite of the hostile environment, he felt more disturbed about his inward struggle than the outward threat to his life. Trying to resist the mental pull back to the field hospitals, he closed his eyes momentarily to clear his mind. When he opened them, he saw Penn lying on the table before him.

"What do ya need, Yank?" Matthew hollered, bringing Gideon back to the present.

"I need fresh water, a sharp knife, alcohol, a needle, thread, something for bandages, more light," Gideon responded distantly.

CHAPTER TWELVE

Standing on the front porch of the abandoned Timmons place, Josiah watched the rain while Tom Coulter and his brother Ned built a fire in the hearth inside the old farmhouse. Although the Coulter brothers had volunteered to ride with Josiah, the rain had become a downpour, forcing them to stop temporarily at the vacant homestead.

Impatient with the delay, Josiah knew any minute could mean death for the Yankee since the antisocial Bunches had been looking for vengeance for their brother Abel's death for a long time. As Josiah dismally regarded the rain, he knew Abigail was counting on a successful rescue. At this point, however, it seemed doubtful he would get to the Bunch cabin in time.

Staring through the downpour to a meadow

just beyond the homestead, Josiah soberly recalled Abigail's anxious face on the porch when the Bunches had ridden past with the Yankee. Although acknowledging things had gotten complicated since the Northerner had shown up, he still felt Abigail might change her mind about Gideon in time. Once Gideon recovered, perhaps the two of them would be on more equal footing to vie for her affections. Holding to that hope, Josiah focused again on the rain.

"We have needed the rain, Lord, but if you want us to save that man, You're going to have to give me a little help and keep him alive till we get there."

* * *

Tracing the trickling raindrops on the parlor window with her finger, Abigail mused on the Bunch brothers' hatred exhibited earlier. As a sudden wave of hopelessness enveloped her, Nathan entered the parlor and pulled her to him, sensing her despair.

"If only we heard, Uncle Nathan. If only we knew they got there in time," she cried plaintively, burying her face in his suit jacket.

"Abigail, Providence brought Gideon to us. I find it hard to believe God would go to all that bother just to let him die at the hands of the Bunches. Have faith. The Lord has not slept either this past night. He works in strange ways sometimes, but He knows what He is doing."

Past dawn, the sky still held its darkness as the rain continued to pour. Hearing a knock on the front door, Nathan left the parlor as Abigail followed.

"Nathan, I saw your light. Guess we won't be fishing this morning," Jeremiah Johnson, Braxton Springs' minister, greeted pleasantly on the porch after Nathan opened the door.

"Can you sit a spell, Jeremy? We could use your help," Nathan invited.

"All right, Nathan," Jeremy responded, noting Nathan's worried expression as he shook the rain off his coat and entered the house.

Lingering by the open door, Abigail stared at the downpour.

"Please, Lord, Gideon has been through so

much. Bring him back to us. Help Josiah get there in time," she implored.

* * *

After successfully extracting the bullet and bandaging Martha's wound, Gideon fell into an uneasy dozing on the bench by his patient. Drifting in and out of nightmarish visions, he finally awoke with a start. Noting Sarah, Chauncey, and Seth asleep across from him at the table, he turned his attention to Martha.

"How's ma sister? Will she make it?" Matthew interjected from the hearth.

Glancing back to him, Gideon frowned at the rifle trained on him and pushed down against the table to help his aching body rise, waking Sarah in the process.

Rising to her feet, she regarded her seemingly lifeless daughter and glanced to Gideon.

"Do ya remember, Yank, what I tole ya 'bout ma Martha here? Ya were told ta save her life."

Staring blankly at the irate woman for a moment, he peered down at Martha himself, his eyes becoming more intent as he noted with concern the girl certainly seemed lifeless. He leaned over her to check her breathing.

"She is alive," he reported.

Disbelieving, Sarah's face reflected her skepticism. When he moved to check Martha's wound, she grabbed his arm.

"Don't touch her. You've done enough."

Awakened by the conversation, Seth and Chauncey rose to their feet and joined their mother next to Gideon.

"Martha?" Seth called expectantly.

Getting no response, Seth angrily glanced up to Gideon while the other Bunches issued him equally hostile expressions.

Sensing the hopelessness of his situation, Gideon wearily sank down onto the bench.

"Hang 'im," Sarah ordered. "I'll not have any more wild bullets in this place. Hang 'im now."

With eyes widening, Gideon did not resist

when Seth and Chauncey grabbed his arms and hauled him up onto his feet. Wanting the ordeal to end, he compliantly allowed them to drag him out of the cabin and across the yard to a weathered wagon. As Seth tied his hands behind his back up on the wagon bed, the sun broke through the clouds, turning the puddles in the yard into scattered mirrors. While Gideon absently observed the shimmery effect, Matthew hitched a horse to the front of the wagon.

Resigned to his fate, Gideon pictured Tom and their Ohio farm he would never see again. When he dropped his gaze to the wagon bed, he recalled Abigail's concerned expression in the Lawrence kitchen and allowed himself the comfort of her image while Seth threw one end of a rope over the tree branch overhead, baptizing him in a shower of rainwater from the dripping leaves above.

Tilting his head back, Gideon received the drenching absolution as Seth created a noose and slipped it around his neck. Suppressing panic, Gideon swallowed hard as Seth jumped off the wagon and grabbed the other end of the rope, tying it securely around a tree.

"Ready?" Matthew hollered.

Seth nodded, but Chauncey lingered in the wagon, struck by Gideon's seeming calm.

"If ya know any prayers, Yank, ya best be sayin' 'em," Chauncey taunted, hoping to rile him.

"Git down from there, Chauncey," Matthew ordered.

As Chauncey complied, Gideon struggled to loosen his hands, the noose holding him erect.

"Ma, ya want to see this?" Matthew called.

Getting no response, Matthew glanced toward the cabin.

"Ma?" he called again.

The cabin door opened.

Moving into the doorway, Sarah soberly left the cabin and strode across the porch, her dark calico dress complementing the somber occasion. When she anchored in her rocker, she eyed Gideon with contempt. Irritated by his seeming calm, she clenched her jaw and glanced back momentarily to the cabin's open doorway before finally nodding to Matthew.

"Git on with it," she ordered sullenly.

With a nod Matthew complied, turning back to the horse. Hearing a gun fire, he glanced to the wagon and saw Gideon falling onto the wagon bed. Trying to process the perplexing turn of events, he and his brothers glanced quizzically toward the woods, scanning the trees for the shooter. To their dismay Caleb emerged from the woods, his gun reloaded. Undaunted, Sarah rose from her rocker and glanced around her for a gun as Josiah and the Coulter brothers rode into the yard.

Spying Gideon, Josiah slipped off his horse and climbed up onto the back of the wagon. When he heard a cry from inside the cabin, he and the others glanced responsively toward the cabin doorway.

Forgetting Gideon, Sarah hastened inside while the brothers stared anxiously toward the cabin, held in place by Caleb's trained rifle.

"Is he shot, Josiah?" Tom Coulter asked, climbing up onto the wagon seat and grabbing the reins.

"No, Tom. Just the rope," Josiah replied, holding up the severed end of the noose.

With eyes widening, Tom glanced across the yard to Caleb.

"He isn't responding, Tom," Josiah reported. "We best get him to Doctor Lawrence."

Shaking the reins responsively, Tom drove the wagon out of the yard as Ned followed with the horses. When they were gone, Caleb finally lowered his gun, releasing the brothers to join their sister.

CHAPTER THIRTEEN

Dozing in the chair next to Gideon's bed, Abigail stirred when her uncle entered the room.

"You need to lie down awhile, Abigail. I will sit with him," he directed softly. "I will call you when he wakes."

Reluctantly leaving her chair, she paused by the bed and gently pushed Gideon's hair up out of his eye.

Gideon stirred responsively.

"Uncle Nathan?" she called, beckoning to him.

As Nathan drew up beside her, Gideon opened his eyes.

"I am alive," Gideon stated with surprise.

Nathan nodded.

"You are very much alive, son."

Gideon's eyes widened.

"How did I get here?" he asked, noting his familiar surroundings.

"Yesterday Josiah and the Coulter brothers drove you here in the wagon from the Bunch cabin," Nathan replied.

"We were so worried for you, Major," Abigail interjected.

Gideon touched his throat.

"I must say from what I remember, I was a might worried myself. Then there was this shot."

"Caleb's," Nathan confirmed with a nod. "His shot severed the rope above your head. Josiah and the Coulter brothers said they never saw anything like it. Caleb saved your life, Gideon."

"Again? He seems to be my guardian angel, Nathan."

"Yes, Someone up there is looking out for you," Nathan concurred. "Abigail, you want to fetch Gideon some of that soup Mary Stevens sent over? It will help him get his strength back."

With a nod Abigail headed to the door as Gideon's eyes followed her. Noting Gideon's focus,

Nathan anchored in the chair with a smile.

"Is Caleb here, Nathan?" Gideon asked after Abigail's departure.

Nathan shook his head.

"He stopped by briefly to see what shape you were in but left right afterward. What with all the hoopla going on in this town about you, he couldn't take all the bother."

"Hoopla?"

"Yes, Gideon, you are the talk of the town. The mercantile gossip mill will be busy with your story for a long time. Folks are very grateful for what you did for Jed Coulter."

"It wasn't anything anyone else wouldn't have done for the boy," he replied uncomfortably.

Nathan regarded him a moment.

"You sell yourself mighty cheap, Gideon. Many a man would have thought of himself first if he had been in your situation."

"What about the girl?"

"Why, that is the best part, Gideon. Martha Bunch has pulled through and is going to be fine, thanks to you. It has made Sarah Bunch eat pretty humble pie, seeing you saved her daughter's life. That is a hard pill for her to swallow."

"That is impossible, Nathan. I don't know how that girl could have lived. The conditions in that place were downright appalling."

"About like you had in the war?" Nathan responded softly.

Gideon's eyes widened at the reference.

"It was a miracle, I tell you, that she lived, Nathan."

Nathan nodded.

"Maybe so, Gideon. To doctor is to work in the miracle business. One patient lives who seems to have no chance while another one dies when it doesn't even seem that serious. It is a mystery, for sure."

Pausing, Nathan reached into his coat pocket.

"I took the liberty of getting in touch with your brother. I wired him since I felt you might want him to know where you are, Gideon."

"Thanks, Nathan."

"I also told him about my proposal for you to work here with me."

Gideon's face clouded.

"I haven't forgotten what you told me, Gideon, but why don't you see what your brother has to say about it?" Rising from the chair, he handed Gideon the telegram. "I will go see what is keeping Abigail."

As Nathan departed, Gideon glanced down to the folded paper.

* * *

Walking up quietly behind Abigail in the kitchen, Josiah placed a spoon next to the bowl she had placed on the tray, causing her to turn with widening eyes.

"Josiah, it is so good to see you. How can I thank you for saving Major Taylor? It was so brave what you did."

Pleased to be her hero, he grinned.

"You care for him, don't you, Abigail?"

Abigail's eyes widened, surprised by his boldness.

"At first I felt nothing, Josiah. I did not even want him here, as you know. But I would be dishonest if I said I don't feel something for him now. And you mean too much to me to do that."

He bit his lip.

Although disappointed, he had witnessed her affection for Gideon when he and the Coulter brothers had pulled up in front of her house with him in the wagon. Recalling the expression on her face as she ran to the wagon and gazed down at Gideon, he drew in a breath.

"I have known it for a while, Abigail, even before you would acknowledge it to yourself," he shared, fidgeting with the spoon on the tray.

"Then why did you help him like you did?"

"At first it was for you. After I met him and spent some time with him though, it was hard to hate him after that. He seems like a real decent man, especially considering what he did for Jed. Not many men I know would have done that. If he sticks around though, Abigail, I'm not giving up on you that easy."

She smiled.

"Josiah, I don't know what I would do without you. I am sure Major Taylor is very grateful as well."

Josiah returned her smile.

"Actually Caleb and the good Lord should get all the thanks. I'm just grateful God kept him alive till we got there."

"That He did," Nathan interjected with a smile, entering the kitchen.

* * *

Moving gingerly to the chair, Gideon regarded the folded telegram in his lap as a shaft of afternoon sunlight fell across the paper. Appreciative of the light and breeze through the open window, he unfolded the telegram and tilted it toward the light.

Gideon,
Heard about your difficulties. Hope you are better. Consider the doctor's offer since I have help on the farm. Do as you wish. You need to work where needed most.   Tom

Smiling responsively as he finished reading,

Gideon pensively gazed out the window until he heard the bedroom door open. Glancing there, he saw Abigail approaching with his food tray. As he flashed her a warm smile, he placed the telegram aside.

"Thank you, Miss Lawrence," he responded when she placed the tray on his lap.

"It is good to see you up, Major, but do you feel that well?"

"Just to see your face again is the best tonic I could have, Miss Lawrence."

She suppressed a smile.

"Feel up to some company, Major?"

Not waiting for his response, she turned away and motioned toward the doorway.

Curious, he put down his spoon as Jed Coulter entered the room.

"Jed has been wanting to see you since they brought you back in the wagon. You are his hero," she whispered as the boy approached.

"Doctor Taylor," Jed greeted, stopping next to him.

Surprised by the formal address, Gideon's eyes widened.

"I want to thank ya for savin' me from the Bunch brothers."

"Glad I was there to help, Jed."

"Ya could have let those men whip me and gotten away yoreself plumb free," the boy averred with admiration.

"No, Jed, I couldn't have done that. No man could have."

"Well, I'm mighty grateful. And I'm also sorry fer the things I said about ya before the Bunch brothers came. I guess I jest didn't know ya, Doctor Taylor," the boy confessed contritely.

Smiling responsively, Gideon watched with interest as the boy reached inside his pocket and retrieved a white rabbit's foot.

"It's ma favorite thing, Dr. Taylor. I got it huntin' with ma pa. Now I want ya to have it fer luck. Maybe it'll help ya git better faster," he related, placing the treasure in Gideon's hand.

"Thanks, Jed," Gideon replied, moved by the

gift.

"Jed?" a male voice interrupted from the bedroom doorway.

Glancing there, Gideon spied a tall man approaching.

"That's my pa, Doctor Taylor. He helped bring ya back from the Bunches with Josiah and my Uncle Ned."

With an acknowledging nod, Gideon eyed the man gratefully.

"Hope he didn' wear ya out," Tom apologized, stopping next to his son. "We've almost had to tie him down at home to keep 'im away from here."

Gideon smiled.

"Thanks for saving my life at the Bunch cabin. I don't remember a whole lot after hearing the shot."

"It was Caleb. His shot severed the rope. Never seen shootin' like that in ma life."

"And that is the second time Caleb has come to my rescue."

"Thank ya for rescuin' ma boy. I'll always be grateful," Tom related earnestly, extending his hand to Gideon. "Name's Tom Coulter."

"Nice to meet you, Tom. I'm Gideon Taylor," Gideon answered, shaking Tom's hand. "Just glad I was there to help."

CHAPTER FOURTEEN

When Gideon awoke the next morning, he found new pants and a shirt laid out for him on the chair. Surprised by the gifts, he rose and limped to the white ironstone pitcher on the washstand. After washing, he brushed his hair and appreciatively donned his new clothes. When he finally exited his room, he hobbled to the stairs landing and proceeded slowly down the steps, taking one at a time. He was making steady progress when Nathan came out of his office and spotted him.

"I am not sure your knee is up to all that, Gideon," Nathan admonished, helping him down the last steps.

"I just think my leg needs support of some kind. I have been in bed too long, Nathan. I had to get up."

Hearing Gideon's voice, Abigail left the kitchen and entered the hallway, wiping her hands on her apron while Josiah followed.

"What are you doing, Major?" she asked with concern.

"I hope I am no trouble, Miss Lawrence. I just needed to get up and move. Thanks for the new clothes. Where did they come from?"

"I believe you can thank me for that," Josiah answered pleasantly. "The clothes are compliments of the mercantile. When the owners of the store heard who I was getting them for, they just gave them to me."

"Gave them to you?" Gideon asked, his face reflecting his confusion.

"Yeah. Seems like you're the town hero for this week anyway, Gideon," Josiah explained.

"I don't understand."

"Gideon, come into my office," Nathan interrupted. "If I put some splints on that leg, that should give it the support it needs. Josiah, give him a hand."

Obliging Nathan, Josiah helped Gideon into the office and up onto the examining table before retreating with Abigail to the kitchen. As Gideon glanced around him in the office, he noted the neat order to the instruments laid out on a nearby table and the large oak medicine cabinet.

"So this is your office, Nathan," he observed approvingly, eyeing the medicine bottles inside the cabinet.

"Been a doctor here for almost forty years, Gideon," Nathan replied, glancing up momentarily as he applied splints to Gideon's leg.

"Forty years?"

"Thai is why I am planning to retire," Nathan explained, leaving him a moment. "You should be able to get around with these, Gideon," he remarked, retrieving a set of crutches. "Let's go have some breakfast."

With a nod Gideon moved off the examining table and took the crutches.

* * *

After breakfast Josiah left for work at the livery, and Nathan returned to his office so Gideon anchored on the front porch swing with Abigail's assistance to get a good look at Braxton Springs and experience some peace and quiet after his ordeal with the Bunches. Spotting Josiah close to his livery down the street, he also noticed the mercantile directly across from the stable before moving his gaze to the town church across from the Lawrence house. While he focused on the white clapboard building and its small steeple, Abigail retreated into the house to fetch some coffee. When she returned, she handed him a steaming cup and turned away momentarily to gaze at the church herself as he contentedly watched her and sipped his coffee.

"You look nice in those new clothes, Major," she commented finally, turning back to him at last.

Glancing down responsively, he smiled.

"I am grateful for them, Miss Lawrence," he answered sheepishly, "but I would like to pay for them. I am certainly no hero like the people in this town reportedly think."

"You will have a hard time convincing Jed Coulter or Martha Bunch you are not a hero, Major."

Uncomfortable with the praise, he glanced again to the church.

"I think would like to go over there for a little while. Do you think it would be all right?"

"Of course, Major. Do you need help? I could accompany you if you need assistance."

"Thanks for offering, but I need to do this myself," he replied, handing her his cup before grabbing his crutches.

As he made his way down the steps, she watched him a moment before retreating inside the house. Pausing in her uncle's office doorway, she found him watching Gideon through the front window. When he sensed her presence, he turned and smiled.

"Think he will be all right, Uncle Nathan?" she asked as she joined him.

"Yes, Abigail, I think he is going to be fine," he replied, putting an arm around her as they watched Gideon together.

* * *

When Gideon entered the church, he noticed a man praying on the front pew so he turned to leave as the man glanced back to him.

"Please, come in," the older man invited in a deep, resonant voice, rising to his feet.

With a nod to him Gideon complied, joining him at the front of the church.

"I apologize if I disturbed you," Gideon greeted as they exchanged handshakes.

"Oh, no, not at all. You must be Gideon Taylor, the man Nathan Lawrence told me about."

Gideon nodded.

"I am Jeremiah Johnson, the minister here in Braxton Springs. It is so good to finally meet you and see you up and about. You have been through quite an ordeal, Nathan told me. What brings you here?"

"Some unfinished business, I guess."

Jeremy nodded.

"Would you like to sit down?"

"Yes. Thank you, Reverend."

Directing Gideon to the front pew, Jeremy

placed Gideon's crutches on the floor and anchored next to him as Gideon pondered how to begin.

"Would you like me to leave you alone?" Jeremy offered softly, seeing Gideon's gaze fixed on his hands.

"No, Reverend, you don't have to go," Gideon answered, glancing up at the cross above the altar. "I have a lot to be grateful for. There is a mountain man, Caleb, who has saved my life twice."

"Yes, I heard about that. Certainly God's doing, wouldn't you agree, Gideon?"

With a nod Gideon returned his gaze to his hands.

"I was a Federal surgeon during the war, Reverend, and it turned out to be a very dark time. I sensed a distance from God after a friend died at the siege at Chattanooga. Finally I quit talking to God altogether."

Pausing a moment, Gideon drew in a breath.

"I was raised differently. I attended church every Sunday with my family and saw the light when I was ten. I felt bad when I quit talking to God, and the distance just seemed to take me to a even darker place. Since I have come to Braxton Springs though, I have been thinking maybe I was wrong about God, His being so far from me, I mean."

Listening attentively, Jeremy nodded.

"So I was sitting on the Lawrences' swing and saw your church here. I thought maybe it was time I got reacquainted, if you follow my meaning."

Jeremy smiled.

"I certainly don't know everything you have been through, Gideon, but I can tell you God is never distant. We are the ones who create the gap. Even with the Bunch brothers, God was working through all that to bring you here, I think. God works in strange ways and sometimes through strange people to get our feet back on the right road. God loves you, Gideon, and He has never stopped loving you, no matter where your feet have taken you or what you have done."

Moved, Gideon bit his lip and nodded.

CHAPTER FIFTEEN

The next day Gideon decided to accompany the Lawrences to church, not realizing the sensation it would cause. Braxton Springs had been so abuzz with talk about him and his difficulties with the Bunch brothers that the mercantile customers had talked about little else. Even the elderly men seated daily around the store's stove had diligently dissected the topic.

"What would have happened to the Coulter boy if that Yankee hadn't stepped in?"

"That Bunch family has always been trouble. Imagine tryin' to beat a young boy like that."

"Herd the Yank is up and farin' much better."

"Who wouldn't fare much better with Abigail Lawrence attendin' 'im?"

"Yeah, herd the Yank's good lookin' too, so

Josiah better watch out. And he's a doctor."

Additional speculation circulated right before the Sunday service so when Gideon hobbled into the sanctuary on his crutches with the Lawrences and Josiah, people murmured responsively. Oblivious, Gideon focused on moving his crutches down the aisle.

"Good morning, Doctor Taylor," Jed called from his seat on the aisle.

Grateful to see a familiar face, Gideon smiled and paused his crutches by Jed's pew as Tom Coulter, seated beside his son, immediately rose and shook Gideon's hand.

"Dr. Taylor, this is my brother Ned and his family," Tom introduced, motioning to his brother in the pew behind him.

Issuing Ned's wife a respectful nod, Gideon shook Ned's hand and noted for the first time the many faces staring his direction. Leaving the Coulter clan, he continued down the aisle to Nathan waiting beside a front pew. After taking a seat between Abigail and Nathan, Gideon glanced to Josiah seated on Abigail's right. Noting Josiah's smile, Gideon nervously returned it as the minister passed their pew and ascended the platform to begin the service.

When Jeremy motioned to the congregation to rise, Nathan took Gideon's elbow to help him stand while Abigail retrieved a hymnal off the pew to share with him. As the congregation boisterously began to sing, Gideon's eyes widened, having never heard such harmony and singing before. Peering more intently at the hymnal, he saw shapes on the page instead of notes. Intrigued, he opted to listen.

At the end of the hymn singing, Reverend Johnson motioned for all to be seated for prayer.

"We thank you, Lord, for watching over us this week, especially over young Jed Coulter," Jeremy prayed. "We thank you for Dr. Gideon Taylor who risked so much to save Jed."

Surprised, Gideon glanced up a moment before returning his gaze to his hands in embarrassment. When he noticed Abigail's soft chuckle beside him, he glanced to her and noted her auburn curls and silk bonnet as he drank in her lavender scent.

"Finally, Lord, we also thank You for saving Martha Bunch's life through Your instrument of Dr. Taylor here," the reverend continued, garnering Gideon's attention again.

"Help the Bunch family be grateful for the gift You have given them, Lord," Jeremy concluded. "Be with us now. Bless our crops and our homes. Give us a good harvest in the fall. In Jesus' Name, Amen."

"Amen," the congregation echoed.

* * *

After Sunday dinner the men sought respite on the front porch while Abigail lingered in the kitchen. Since Nathan opted for a seat on the porch swing next to Gideon, Josiah anchored comfortably in a wicker chair. Noting an unusual number of people strolling by the house that afternoon, Josiah speculated the townspeople were simply trying to get a closer look at the town hero. When Samuel Evans and his wife Amanda paused by the front gate and openly gawked, Josiah smiled and glanced to Gideon.

"Gideon, the people at the gate are the good folks who gave you the clothes. Samuel and Amanda Evans own the mercantile across from my livery," he explained

"I am much obliged. I would like to pay them, however," Gideon responded, flashing the couple a smile as they left the gate and headed across the street toward the church. "Nathan, I want to ask you about the hymn singing this morning. I have never heard singing like that before."

"Anyone care for some lemonade?" Abigail interjected, placing a refreshment tray on the porch table as the men rose respectfully and issued eager nods.

"It is called harp singing, Gideon," Nathan answered with a smile, glancing back to him as he left the swing to fetch them some lemonade. "People here learn music by shapes, not notes."

"Well, it is quite remarkable, Nathan," Gideon responded, anchoring again on the swing.

"Yes, I think so too, Gideon. I remember the first time I heard it after I had settled in the valley.

Was a long time ago. Just another thing that makes this place special, I think," Nathan replied as Abigail poured lemonade into glasses.

Focused on the beverage distribution, Gideon did not notice a wagon pulling up in front of the house until Nathan returned to the swing and handed him a glass of lemonade. After taking a sip, Gideon looked up and spied Sarah Bunch and her daughter Martha watching him attentively from their wagon while the notorious brothers stared from atop their horses. Drawing in a breath, Gideon began to rise defensively until Nathan's extended arm restrained him, causing Gideon to glance to him quizzically.

"It will be all right, Gideon," Nathan stated, his eyes on the Bunches as well. "Just stay where you are."

Hearing her uncle's comment, Abigail turned toward the uninvited visitors and frowned. As she wrapped an arm around the porch post and glared at the motley family, Josiah noted her focus and took a defensive position beside her on the top porch step.

Across the street at the church gate, Samuel

and Amanda Evans began walking back to the Lawrence house with Reverend Johnson while other townspeople gathered as well in front of the house, keeping a safe distance between themselves and the Bunches since all anticipated trouble.

Seein a crowd forming, Sarah moved to climb down from the wagon so Matthew promptly dismounted to assist her. When she reached the street, she gathered her shawl up around her while Seth and Chauncey helped their sister down from the wagon seat.

Carrying a bouquet of wildflowers, Martha swallowed hard, intimidated by the growing number of spectators. As she accompanied her mother through the Lawrence front gate to the porch, she glanced back to her subdued brothers waiting by the wagon. Drawing in an anxious breath, she returned her attention to her mother who was eyeing Nathan and Gideon on the swing.

"Doc," Sarah greeted curtly.

Nathan nodded with forced politeness as Sarah eyed Gideon with interest.

"I see yore feelin' better, Yank," Sarah observed.

"No thanks to you, Sarah Bunch," Nathan admonished sternly.

With a responsive frown, Sarah glanced away from him and regarded the growing crowd.

"We didn't come here to make no trouble," she announced.

Noting the townspeople's cold stares, she glanced back to Gideon who had dropped his gaze to his hands. Biting her lip pensively, she nodded to her daughter.

"Go ahead, girl," she encouraged.

With eyes widening, Martha complied and approached the porch swing.

"I brought these fer ya. I'm so grateful fer ya savin' my life," the girl relayed softly, garnering Gideon's attention.

Surprised by the gift, he took the flowers and smiled.

"Are you feeling better?" he asked.

Overcome by his attention, Martha nodded to

him and timidly returned his smile.

"I am glad."

Moved by his kind demeanor, she smiled again and returned to her mother as he watched her retreat. When he locked eyes with Sarah, his smile vanished.

"I knowed sorry can't mean much to ya," Sarah remarked, grateful to have his attention at last.

"You have got that right, Sarah Bunch. Not much," Nathan interjected scornfully.

Ignoring him, she waited for Gideon's response. When he gave none, she glanced to the townspeople.

"Well, I'm about to say somethin', and those who know me know I don't say nothin' I don't mean." Tilting her head back, she surveyed the crowd before returning her attention to Gideon. "Ya have my word, Yank, that my boys will never be botherin' ya agin."

Glancing skeptically to the brothers, Gideon watched as their stares dropped collectively to the ground. With a frown he returned his attention to Sarah.

Getting no other response from him, she turned to go, noting for the first time Josiah and Abigail's cold expressions as she gathered her shawl around her and retreated with Martha to the wagon. After her sons helped her back up onto the wagon seat, she glanced back to Gideon standing now on the porch.

"That's all I came here to say, Yank," she called.

"His name is Dr Gideon Taylor, Sarah," Nathan corrected, leaving the swing to stand beside Gideon.

She nodded an acknowledgment.

"Good day then, Dr. Taylor," she concluded before grabbing the reins and motioning to her sons to leave.

After the Bunches departed, Gideon anchored again on the swing, his gaze fixed pensively on his hands as townspeople dispersed before the house.

"I thought I'd seen about everything," Josiah declared with widening eyes after all had left.

With a nod Nathan glanced to him.

"Yes, that was a memory maker," Nathan agreed before finishing the last of his drink. "Any more lemonade, Abigail?"

Grabbing the empty pitcher, she retreated into the house.

"I need to get back to the livery," Josiah remarked, rising and placing his empty glass on the porch table. "I'll stop back later. In the meantime, Gideon, see if you can keep the excitement down here till I get back."

Gideon smiled.

"I will try my best, Josiah."

With a chuckle and a wave Josiah bounded down the porch steps and left.

"Well, Gideon, I would say that just about does it," Nathan remarked.

"What do you mean, Nathan?" Gideon responded, regarding him quizzically.

"I mean, you have nothing keeping you from staying in Braxton Springs now."

Amused by his persistence, Gideon smiled and glanced across the street to the church.

"Well, it is enough to make a man dream, I guess. I don't think I can return to medicine though. You don't know how hard it was for me to help that girl."

Nathan nodded.

"What is important, Gideon, is that you did. That is the beauty of it, you see, the beginning."

Drawing in a breath, Gideon nodded and glanced again to the church.

"The reverend helped me get reacquainted with God yesterday, and I admit I feel a lot more hopeful than I have felt for a long time. He seems to think God has been working through all of this to bring me here, Nathan."

Nodding to him, Nathan glanced back to the door for his lemonade. When he spied his niece eavesdropping inside the screen door, he suppressed a smile as she proceeded sheepishly onto the porch and placed the filled pitcher on the table.

"God works in strange ways sometimes, Gideon," Nathan confirmed as he rose to refill his glass.

"Well, I know a mountain man I need to thank, and I feel I owe a lot to you and Josiah so maybe I could stay awhile and see how things work out. My brother seems fine without me since he has gotten help with the farm."

"I know another reason that will keep you here if medicine won't," Nathan teased, refilling his glass.

Glancing to him quizzically, Gideon noticed Abigail's presence and smiled.

"Yes, Gideon, that something should keep you here for sure," he added, retreating into the house with a chuckle.

Left alone with Gideon on the porch, Abigail shifted her weight uncomfortably as he nervously fingered his empty glass. Descending the porch steps after another awkward moment, she disappeared around the corner of the house.

Surprised by her departure, Gideon grabbed his crutches and followed. When he reached the side of the house, he saw her standing under a stately oak tree, its lofty branches providing a green canopy above her. Encouraged by her smile, he joined her under the tree.

"I was so afraid when the Bunches took you that I would never see you again, Major," she remarked, eliciting his smile. "And then when they showed up here today and apologized, well, it makes me think you might stay."

"Would that be pleasing to you, Miss Lawrence?"

Glancing back over the yard, she absently absorbed the greenery as he waited for her reply. When she returned her attention to him, she smiled.

"Uncle Nathan sure would find it pleasing," she answered evasively.

Unsure how to respond, he glanced down to his feet, his face clouding.

Amused, Abigail pushed the hair up out of his eye, garnering his attention again.

"I would be pleased as well, Major," she confided softly, her eyes inviting and warm.

Glancing up at the leafy labyrinth above them, Gideon struggled to maintain control and distance.

Feeling so unworthy of her, he knew that burdening her with his problems would be unfair, yet he found it difficult to resist the strong impulse to stay with the Bunch brothers pacified and the townspeople open and friendly. Ignoring his reservations, he returned his gaze to her, drawn even more than before.

"Then I will stay, Miss Lawrence," he declared, boldly taking her hands.

Noting her hazel eyes brightening, Gideon leaned in responsively and gave her a kiss.

Witnessing the action from his office window inside the house, Nathan smiled.

"Yes, Lord, You work in strange ways, but You always know what You're doing," he observed softly as he left the window.

Journey Home Series

Long Journey Home

A Second Chance

One More Mile

No More Strings

Kingdom Come

Walking Through the Valley

Green Pastures

The Winds of Change

Valley of Decision

One Final Glimpse Backward

ABOUT THE AUTHOR

Author of the best-seller, *Stella's Sisters; Voices From Moldova,* a non-fiction account of human trafficking, **Nancy Silvers** takes a literary departure from nonfiction with her Journey Home novel series. Mixing her love of history with storytelling, she creates the saga of Gideon Taylor, a Federal surgeon during the Civil War. Nancy resides in Waterville, Ohio.

Script A Life Books

Waterville, Ohio

Scriptalife.com